Heart and Dagger

by

Holland Rae

The Ships in the Night Series

This is a work of fiction. Names, characters, places, and incidents are either the product of the author's imagination or are used fictitiously, and any resemblance to actual persons living or dead, business establishments, events, or locales, is entirely coincidental.

Heart and Dagger

Cover Art by *Debbie Taylor*

The Wild Rose Press, Inc.
PO Box 708
Adams Basin, NY 14410-0708
Visit us at www.thewildrosepress.com

Publishing History
First Tea Rose Edition, 2017
Print ISBN 978-1-5092-1806-6
Digital ISBN 978-1-5092-1807-3

The Ships in the Night Series
Published in the United States of America

He could have been her husband
these years now, had he ever written back, had he not turned himself away from everything London and Paris were to him. He had been a coward and fool.

And yet, the knowledge did not serve to calm his temper in the slightest. Instead, he nearly ground his teeth to dust, as she continued her even speech.

"I have never needed a man to care for me," she said, her gaze so full of disdain, Armand felt himself growing smaller in the wake of it. "I have never needed anyone to care for me." This time, when she spoke, there was no denying the sadness that filtered through her words, or the expression in her eyes, and Armand felt his own grief in it, felt his own sadness as it mirrored hers.

"Why are you trying to change me?" she asked him. He knew he needed to back down, knew that if he spoke right at this moment, as this woman stood before him in her britches, then he would regret it forever. He knew all these things, and yet the anger seemed to consume him, anger, fear, sadness.

"It's about time someone tried."

Dedications

To Mahesh.
You are now officially a romance novel hero.
You always were, and always will be, my dear friend.
~*~
To Robbie.
My eternal source of inspiration and support.
~*~
To Bill.
You were the inspiration for my Captain Dwyer
and for so much love in this world.
We know you're still with us.

Prologue

16 April 1793
London townhouse of the Earl of Derby

"I'm going to marry him." Charlotte Talbot, eldest daughter of the Earl of Derby, threw herself upon her silk coverlet and allowed her hair to come loose from its perfect coif in an overt display of unladylike behavior. Her sister, Lady Elizabeth Talbot, younger by three years and, though only twelve, often considered the wiser of the Talbot children, raised a delicate eyebrow.

"Whom, exactly, do you presume to marry?" Eliza inquired, her tone not without reproach. It would be unkind to imply that Lady Charlotte Talbot was the type of young woman prone to dramatic exclamation regarding her future matrimonial prospects. Eliza, however, was her sister, and because siblings were given the distinct privileges of being unkind to one another, Charlotte was *precisely* the type of young woman prone to dramatic exclamation regarding her future matrimonial prospects.

Eliza loudly and often placed the blame for Charlotte's behavior on their mother, or rather, lack thereof, whom she had known just three short years, before a carriage accident had taken her life and permanently wounded her father, Lord Richard Talbot,

1

Earl of Derby, in the process. Ladies who were raised by their mothers, and not the flitting about of servants, nannies, and governesses, were far more likely to behave in a way befitting their stature. To the dismay of said servants, nannies, and governesses, as well as the elder sister gazing longingly to the ceiling above her bed, Eliza had managed to get her hands upon a copy of Florence Pennywig's *A Lady's Guide to Moral Behavior*, from which she had been quoting, rather impolitely, thought most on the receiving end, to any unfortunate soul who dared to defy Miss Pennywig's proper moral code.

Charlotte, who couldn't give a fig for the notions brought forth by Miss Pennypig, as she had taken to calling her simply to spite her younger sister, was ignoring Eliza. It was one matter to have an audience to your dramatic exclamation regarding future matrimonial prospects, but quite another entirely to have said exclamations questioned.

The truth of it was, she was certain she *would* be marrying this particular gentleman, given that their fathers had been the best of companions since their school days, spending their youth on country estates a stone's throw from one another and raising their offspring in the same manner. She had grown up beside him, quite literally. Now that she was a young woman, however, and starting to see him for something other than the boy who lived next door for her whole life—well, she had little doubt that their two fathers would do all in their power to see them wedded.

Lady Armand Rajaram de Bourbon. It was a mouthful of a name, but so much more worldly than simple Charlotte Talbot, daughter of the Earl of Derby.

Truly, her family reeked of the British peerage. Armand, as she had known him all her young life, was son to a man who held titles in both England and in France, and to a woman whose family harkened back to the oldest monarchs in the vast and unknown land of India. Her own family, for the last six hundred years, had traveled as far as Suffolk, and perhaps West Yorkshire, but Charlotte had certainly never been on a ship out at sea for several months, daring the elements to come and take her, as she traveled to new lands.

Lord and Lady de Bourbon, known in England for their earldom of Devon, had seen the world around, including Armand in several of their epic adventures. It wouldn't have mattered, Charlotte considered, if they had only been as far as Paris and Rome—that still boasted a lifetime of miles from her own London and countryside homes.

As Armand's wife, she would travel the world. Her mind slipped back into the romantic whispers of young love. She had heard tales of open seas, of water creatures twice the size of horses, of islands where it never, ever rained. They could visit the land of Armand's mother, which she had glimpsed through the colorful gowns and sparkling jewels worn by Lady de Bourbon. Her fingers and ears shone in bright firelight, twinkling with rubies and emeralds and gold. Perhaps Armand would take her, Charlotte, there one day.

Eliza's voice, in the true nature of younger sisters, came cutting through with a tone so grating that, try as she might, Charlotte could not ignore it.

"I said, whom exactly do you think you're going to marry?" her sister repeated, the hints of a petulant child still discernible throughout her recently highly polished tone.

Charlotte sat up in the bed and threw a tufted pillow at her, enjoying the squeak she made before ducking off to the side and tumbling from the chair onto the floor. Now, what would Miss Florence Pennypig have to say about *that* kind of behavior?

"Armand," she told Eliza, when her sister had deigned to sit back down, fluffing her hair as though it were that of a true lady, and not the simple braids worn by young girls still in the schoolroom.

Eliza, much to Charlotte's chagrin, snorted in a way positively forbidden by *A Lady's Guide to Moral Behavior.*

"You're going to marry *Armand?*" she asked, obviously unable to keep the incredulity from her tone. "As in, our Armand?"

Precisely the same. They had grown up, both in the countryside and in their London townhouses, as friends and required playmates. More often than not, Armand, two years her senior, and Charlotte would sneak off, trying to lose Eliza and Armand's brother, Henri, Eliza's age to the month, in the vast orchards that covered the land upon both of their country estates. As young children, they had climbed trees and rooftops, until nannies and nursemaids had nearly fainted at the sight of them. As older children, they had even shared tutors, so close was the friendship between their fathers.

Charlotte, though it pained her deeply to admit, could empathize with some of her sister's confusion. After all, the boys of the de Bourbon family were near as cousins or brothers to them. Was it not strange, then, to find herself quite suddenly declaring plans of matrimony to one, some years before even entering the

4

marriage mart?

But things had been changing between them, Charlotte knew. It hadn't been an immediate evolution, barely a noticeable one at all. They had begun dressing in proper attire to visit the other, begun calling each other by, if not title, then at least full name.

"He's practically our brother, Charlotte," Eliza said now, her voice a trifle alarmed. "It's tantamount to marrying within your immediate family." Charlotte raised an eyebrow, and Eliza relaxed back into her chair a little. "All right, it's not quite so bad as all that, but be serious."

It was an amusing thought, indeed, that the young men of the de Bourbon family could ever be mistaken for blood relatives to the Talbot girls. Their skin, a gift from their beautiful mama, was so much darker than her own. It was a deep, almost toasted brown, that gave one the impression that Armand and Henri spent their days in the sun, whereas she and Eliza could quite easily be mistaken for pieces of ivory. And Armand's hair...Her dreamy sighs returned, as she thought of the dark, deep black hair that had been growing more unruly by the day, though he did his best to tie it back. She found herself wondering if his hair was quite as soft as it looked, and why her own hair, equally as dark but nowhere near as beautiful a shade of brown, had the effect of making her appeal a great dealer paler, where as his only served to make him look more rugged— well, as rugged as a boy of seventeen might look.

"I *am* being serious. Today, in the gardens..." She blushed, not for the first time that day, as she recalled the way he had looked at her, recalled the sensation of their nearness that would have scandalized anyone, had she been properly debuted. "He told me I looked beautiful today." Charlotte sighed again and flushed anew at the words, as they sent a shiver of pure joy coursing through her. "Armand has never, ever seen a thing I've worn, Eliza. You know that." Her sister's lack of response was agreement enough. "He said I looked beautiful." Charlotte leaned back into her coverlet and sighed. She could hardly wait to get married.

****

2 May 1793
London townhouse of the Earl of Derby

There was no use crying anymore. And since there was no use crying, her body should simply stop the ridiculous, embarrassing activity at once. Though her eyes were bloodshot and her sheets stained, more tears still streamed down her face, over the coverlet, and across the white parchment sitting upon her lap, growing increasingly difficult to read with each drop that smeared the inky words.

Eliza sat beside her in the bed. Though she had yet to abandon her crusade for the advantages of the works of Miss Florence Pennywig, she had been kind enough to temporarily forgo the effort, in favor of trying to soothe Charlotte, to whatever extent she could be soothed, which truly wasn't much at all.

Armand, along with Henri and the Earl of Devon and his wife, was gone. Not two days prior, Armand had bid her farewell from the docks, placed a chaste kiss to her trembling fingers, and promised to write as often as was possible. His mother was ill. The once beautiful Lady de Bourbon was growing gaunt, her skin sinking sallow into her bones. If they did not leave immediately, Armand had explained, they would not make it in time for her to see her family. As it was, they were likely too late.

Charlotte knew she should have wept for Lady de Bourbon, the woman who had been a constant in her life, near as a mother would have been, for so many years. But to her, the earl's wife had always been reminiscent of a precious china figurine. She was elegant, beautiful, sparkling in the sun and shining in the firelight, but she was fragile, built on a foundation of glass and precious stone.

Instead, she wept for the loss of her closest friend. Armand had not promised to return. Even the normally loquacious Henri had looked silently upon them, as they waved goodbye from the ship. It was possible, Charlotte thought bitterly, that she would never see any of them again.

It was difficult for her to believe that only a fortnight had passed since the time she had promised herself, if not him, that they would one day wed. The fantasy, as brief as it had been, was a glorious one, and in a moment of dreadfully moist weakness, Charlotte sobbed for the loss of that as well. Since she would likely never even *see* Armand again, it was even more likely she would never marry him. At the thought, and the encroaching realization that, at some point soon, she would have to marry *someone*, Charlotte broke back into a fit of sobs.

Eliza, for all she was a pest of a younger sister, rubbed her back and offered her sips of tea.

"It will be all right," she whispered, her voice back to its usual, loving cadence, none of Miss Pennywig's flummery added in. "I promise, darling, it will be all

7

right."

But Charlotte, prone as she was to dramatic exclamations regarding her future matrimonial prospects and many other things, truly could not see how a life without Armand Rajaram de Bourbon, eldest son of the Earl of Devon, her once future-husband, could possibly be all right.

Chapter One

Ten years later, 14 April 1803
300 leagues off the coast of the Americas

Captain of the *Liberté*, part-time smuggler, full-time mercenary, Catalina Sol woke from her dream with such force she nearly spilled the small pot of ink at the edge of her desk. She had fallen asleep while working again, the sway of the ship in the open seas making her once-sharp focus lilt. It was not the first time in a fortnight when she had woken precariously close to a desk as wet and murky black as the sea itself.

And what the devil kind of dream had she been having, anyway? Catalina Sol was a fierce captain, fearsome, to hear certain folks tell of it. She defended her people to the very edge of the earth, and in seven years upon the open ocean, she had made a reputation for herself that once upon a time would have made her papa faint dead away.

Her family now consisted of one sister, far away, far, far away, making a name for their family as she, Catalina, had never done, and the lost souls who had drifted toward the *Liberté*, sure as she had upon the *Starling* all those years ago. She liked this life; it was a life she had worked hard for, one she would defend with her final breath.

What was she doing then, dreaming of the past?

9

Her life now was just the way she had always wanted it to be, free, unencumbered by the strictures of a society that asked too much, without ever asking what it was that *she* had wanted. Until she left England in the dead of night, no one had ever asked her what she wanted.

The dream was not, much to Catalina's chagrin, melting from the corners of her mind like grains of sand in an endless hourglass. Instead, the more she thought on it, the more the edges sharpened and refined themselves, until she could all but picture her bedchamber in her father's London townhouse ten years ago. She had cried herself silly for a month over the leaving of her dearest friend in the world. And then she had run.

Well, Catalina corrected herself, it hadn't happened precisely like that. Lord Richard Talbot, Earl of Derby and her father in a former life, had confessed his plan to wed her to the oldest son of his closest friend. It had hardly been a matter to be confessed, however. She and Eliza had known it was coming from the time they could spell their own names, and she had been one of the lucky ones who had anticipated matrimony and coming of age with excitement, rather than fear.

But then, then Armand had left, and she had stayed. Well, that was how it always was in the novels. Catalina rubbed the sleep from her eyes. And if her story had followed the plot of a novel, it certainly had a villain. Lord Chatwin Poppet had been twice the age she had been, when he offered for her hand. She had barely been eligible a fortnight, and his beady eyes had narrowed upon her vulnerable naiveté with the skill of a hungry vulture.

Even then, even as simply the elder Talbot

daughter of the Earl of Derby, Catalina had known that she could not commit herself to a lifetime as the wife of Lord Poppet, with his overly friendly, impolite fingers, and his leering glances. It hadn't been, however, until he had raised his cane to her one evening, only narrowly missing the curve of her cheek, that Catalina Sol had truly understood just how far she would go to escape his plans for marriage and, as she was later to learn, his desire for her dowry, for not only had the man been as nasty as a rat, but his affinity for cards and birds of paradise had left him as poor as a beggar's wife.

It was oddly amusing to think upon it now, Catalina considered, taking a moment to peer at the familiar illustration upon the far wall—the map was nearly ten years old and showed its age. When she had first set out to sea, that map would have served her well, but now it did little more than hang as a relic, a reminder of how quickly time passed—had passed since the very first time she'd needed her own map for her own ship. Why, new countries seemed to be cropping up at an alarming rate, these days. It was very nearly humorous to think that at the ripe age of just eighteen, she'd donned a riding cloak and slipped out in the middle of the night, bound for the docks. A young lady of the peerage who had never once been in any body of water deeper than a washing tub, and she had chosen the docks. Fear and desperation had ruled her that night, emotions she had honed into sharp-edged friends that were never far from her side, better weapons than any rapier or pistol, when properly controlled.

There was a knock on the door, and Catalina called

for entry. A young boy, just thirteen to the month, opened it and allowed a woman heavy with child to precede him into the room.

"Captain, Miss McEwan wanted to know when we might be seeing land," he said, his voice cracking upon the last word. Catalina looked at him and felt a sense of intense fondness. When she had first met young William, he'd been naught but a child, and now he was on this side of manhood and doing it proud, if she did say so. Another reminder of the speed of time, when one was looking in the other direction. Disregarding her nostalgia and the cobwebs of memories, she turned to face the aforementioned Miss McEwan.

"Is your stomach feeling upset?" she asked the girl, indicating to William, who slipped through the door without another word. Rose McEwan nodded, though from one glance at the sickly white hue of her face, Catalina knew the answer.

"Every hour or so, I feel as though I'm to lose my meal," the young girl mumbled, though it was clearly an effort on her part to speak. Rose McEwan was barely seventeen—the second daughter of a sheep farmer from the Americas. She had been unwed and had only just learned of her delicate situation, before fleeing for the docks in search of the notorious Catalina Sol.

"We'll be docking at Dwyer House in just a few days' time," Catalina said, an entirely true note of sympathy to her voice. Though she'd never, herself, been in a family way, she had witnessed many women who had. Their experiences upon dry land had been enough to put her off the matter. To be aboard a ship on the open ocean was likely too much of a test.

"I thank ye, Captain," Rose said, and it looked to

Catalina as though she were using the whole of her strength to speak. This was no shrinking violet, even for her young age. She had done what she had to, in order to protect her unborn babe. That she appeared only mildly discomforted was a testament to her strength. The young girl took another breath. "I haven't much to give ye in the way of thanks, and I know I've been an awful burden upon the crew these months."

Catalina held up her hand to stop her. It was a speech she had heard before, from so many. "You have been no burden, and neither has the child," she said, kindly but firmly. "And you will be no burden at Dwyer House either. You will have a life there, as will your babe, and that is payment enough to myself and the crew." It was barely discernible, but Catalina would testify that she saw a shade of color return to the girl's cheeks. "Now, you rest. Tell William I've recommended you root of ginger and whatever dry bread remains in the cupboards. Sleep these next days, and we'll be on land well before your time." Rose nodded, giving her thanks once more, and then taking her leave.

She'd be damned if she ever regretted leaving England. Surely, she and her sister remained in the best communication possible for a woman at sea, and if returning was what she truly wished to do, then Catalina would find a way to make it possible. Hell, she could return to the life of Lady Charlotte Talbot if that was her desire, marry a man for whom she cared, live out the rest of her days upon an estate, and bring an end to her life at sea. But it was no longer her life that was at stake. It hadn't been a matter of simply her own life since she had first bought the *Liberté* and felt the cool grip of a sword in her hand. It hadn't been her life since she had first opened Dwyer House, placed it in the charge of Mrs. Antonia Clarence, and begun a rescue mission that would take her around the world. For every Rose McEwan they safely delivered to Dwyer, two more women waited to take her place. For every William Fischer, there were four more babes in arms, simply waiting at the dock with hope.

She had hope too. Visiting Dwyer and giving Rose McEwan a stable ground upon which to birth her child was only one of the reasons she had turned the ship for Hispanolia. It had been her home from the start, and the inhabitants of Dwyer House had grown each time she returned, as word of the strange captain and crew of *Liberté* spread around the seas. Yes, she had returned for a report from Antonia and to bring Rose to her new home so she might deliver her child on solid land. But she also returned for a far more prudent cause—they needed the money.

Of course, no one on the *Liberté* or at Dwyer House ever lacked for anything. Catalina ensured the very best for her crew of runaways and vagabonds and all those she had set up on land. Once a person was firmly secured in their new home, Antonia and her ladies taught them a craft or a trade, and the sales from such items kept them all in good stead, as well as giving them skills, for if they ever wished to venture from their family at Dwyer. It didn't hurt any that Catalina happened to run a successful trade business as well, peddling their items alongside silks and spices. But she needed more than just good money, and it couldn't be funds drawn from the pot for Dwyer or the *Liberté*.

She was going to open a new home, a second house

for the lost souls of the world. She and Antonia discussed it each time she returned home, and Catalina knew that it would not be long before the current place stood full to capacity. It was time to consider the future, and for that she needed a job.

While crafting and cooking was as fine a way as any to keep the coffers full, a far more businesslike venture ensured her success as a mercenary for the needy. Because, for all that the mismatched crew of the *Liberté* appeared as little more than women with children and young boys, they were a fighting force that could best any pirate crew in the entire sea. Catalina would know—she had taught them all herself, having learned at the hand of a master swordsman. And so they hired themselves out, mercenaries of a sort, for a fantastical price to those who could afford it and for free to those who needed. Right now, it was she who needed a fantastical sum of money to finance her next project.

Catalina turned back to her earlier thoughts. Home and the day that Armand de Bourbon had left for India were far away memories now. It wasn't unusual for them to crop up around this time of year, and though one day they might be more faded in her mind, she would simply have to live with their strange anniversary. Instead of remorseful, Catalina thought, as she left the captain's quarters for the deck, she should be grateful. After all, if Armand had stayed, she would have married him, and where would that have left the Rose McEwans of the world?

The deck was dazzling, alight with all the delicious sun of a Caribbean springtime, as it bounced from the boards being washed by strong young men. She got her fair share of thieves and vagabonds, but over the years, Catalina had learned how to weed out the good eggs from the bad and the ones who liked to think they were bad but were really good at heart. No. She didn't miss anything about England, except the company of her sister. But times were good upon the *Liberté*, and she would never lack for those to love, and those who loved her in return. The strays and runaways she took in were her family now, and she was theirs.

Chapter Two

19 April 1803
400 leagues off the coast of the Americas

Armand Rajaram de Bourbon, Earl of Devon, Comte de Dreux, and son of an Indian princess, had a headache that would rival the morning after of any pirate or vagabond who ever roamed the Spanish Main. He was certain he could hear the waves of blood beating in his ears, as if he were standing upon the shore at high tide.

"Read the letter again." He rarely raised his voice, but even he could not deny the sharp tone that spoke to the room at large. Harrington, a weedy man with glasses standing just to his right, cleared his throat and spoke, his voice wavering slightly.

"To the Right Honorable, The Earl of Devon," Harrington began. Armand winced. There was no doubt in his mind that the phrase *honorable* implied otherwise. "If you wish to see your brother, the second son of the Earl of Devon, Henri de Bourbon, ever again, we request you adhere to these demands." Armand rubbed his eyes, but the pounding in his head only grew worse. He knew it was unlikely to abate any time soon.

"One, cease all capture and imprisonment of pirates. Two, release all pirates from imprisonment immediately. Three, cease all trade in, sale, and distribution of silk, spice, and rum immediately. Adhere strictly to these demands, and your brother will be returned to you alive." Armand had already seen the scrap of parchment upon which the demands had been laid out. He had turned it over in his hand a dozen times, first quickly, in desperation, and then slowly, in hope. He asked, despite knowing the answer, "Is there anything else on the page?"

Harrington looked like a small bird frightened by a dog, and Armand apologized, schooling his tone. "I need time to think," he said after a moment. He dismissed several of the men from the room, leaving a small circle of Harrington and two others, Wendell and Spritz, standing before his desk.

Armand took a glance at the paper again and stood from his chair, pacing over to the window. He had received the missive late the night before. The courier had given no indication as to who had given him the letter and whether he was still upon the island. Since then, Armand had read it over more times than he could remember, until the ink had started to drip before his eyes and his vision had swum. He needed a glass of something strong.

"What are our choices?" Armand asked. Ever since the death of their father, their remaining parent, he and Henri had been as close as brothers came. While much of the pounding at his temple could be attributed to fears for his trade business, or the fears of a magistrate for the future of justice, his heart was feeling the sickness in equal measure.

"We could shut down the trade, release the prisoners, and never arrest another pirate," Wendell put in. He had spent several decades in service to the

King's Royal Navy, and he was a man who took no nonsense from anyone, often including Armand. From the tone of his voice, it was clear that he was as likely to follow a single one of those requests as he was to don a corset and prance through the streets of London.

"I say, sir," Harrington exclaimed, his voice ripe with overexcitement. "How dare you jest at a time like this? We are in the very midst of an emergency."

"All I need is a crew and some cannon," Wendell replied. "Then we won't be in the midst of an emergency anymore." Before his two advisors could further delve into squabbles, Armand cut into the fray.

"It hardly matters. We don't even know who sent the demands, let alone who to threaten with cannon. Perhaps step one should be something related to that, do you not agree, gentlemen?" Wendell looked as though he were close to knocking Harrington's spectacles to the ground, but both men knew a higher authority when it stared them in the face.

"If I might, sir," came the restrained voice of the man not yet involved in their squabble. Spritz had lost one eye in a battle with a band of pirates when he was not yet twenty. Coupled with a long, gray beard and a wise expression that seemed to accompany his deep blue, singular gaze, he gave the impression of knowing more about the world at large than anyone else Armand had ever met. Spritz was a damned good advisor to have on a rock in the middle of the world. "I do have one idea that might protect your interests at both ends." There was a weighty pause as all attention in the room slowly turned toward him.

"Out with it, man," Wendell barked.

Armand quelled him with a glance. "What plan do

you have?" he asked. He was beginning to feel a slight panic settling in. Nearly a whole day had already passed since his brother had been kidnapped from his very own home, one of the most guarded places on the entire island. If they didn't act soon, Armand had little doubt that it would be far too late.

"I overstep my bounds by requesting you keep your mind open," Spritz said. "The plan, at least initially, does not fit within the set of rules you live by."

Armand raised an eyebrow. It was not an uncommon sensation, with Spritz, to feel as though the Holy Father himself had descended to teach man of his own frailties.

"My mind is open," Armand reassured him, albeit, with ferocity. "What is this plan of yours to retrieve my brother?"

Spritz looked him square in the eyes, his single eye seeing well into Armand's mind. It was a disconcerting sensation. "Catalina Sol."

If Armand had believed his head to be pounding before, he had been sorely mistaken. Ten years ago, as their family had sailed to bring their mother back to her homeland one last time, pirates had overrun their ship. Armand had sailed the world several times by the ripe age of seventeen, and his defenses were down. His sword was in his chambers. The pirates stole, fought, and killed. In the end, after tying down all the men and stealing anything of value to be taken off the ship, they set fire to the boards, threw a few bottles of rum against the flame, and jumped for safety to the waters below, swimming back to their ship.

His mother, though she had been so terribly weak, untied them. With the help of the other women aboard the ship, the men were released into the blazing flame of the deck. Armand remembered each moment of that morning as though it were happening again, right before his eyes. He screamed to his brother and father to jump to the waters below, bellowed, his voice hoarse above the flame. And then he turned to his mother.

He remembered her expression with a glassy sheen, as though the memory cabinet of his mind took out her final smile, washed it with love and nostalgia, and showered it in a sprinkle of well-fed guilt.

"My son…" Her voice was so soft, so very soft he was barely able to hear it over the din. "My son." She pointed to the vast ocean, where not a single island or ship appeared against the horizon, and Armand's stomach dropped into his knees.

"You have to come," he told her, even as every impetuous bone in his body acknowledged the horrible truth.

"I am not strong enough," she said, and the serene smile that slipped gently across her beautiful, gaunt face told Armand that she had already made her peace. He hadn't.

"Mama—" The name he hadn't called her since he had been a babe in arms. "Mama, you must come with us." Perhaps it was selfish to ask. He had often wondered. The truth of it was always going to end with her slipping out of his fingers. But he had been robbed—their whole family had been robbed—of the last weeks, perhaps last days, they were going to spend with her, of her final thoughts and expressions of love. He didn't give a damn that their every belonging had been stolen. Far worse was the theft of their final days with his mama.

"Please keep your brother safe."

Armand nodded, feeling a thousand miles away.

"Now go, my son," she whispered, cupping his cheek. The fire grew closer now, and he knew that their time was short, shorter than he had ever imagined it would be.

"Mama," he repeated. "Please come with us."

Her eyes answered for her, and Armand wondered whether she was even seeing what was happening around her anymore.

"I love you, my son..." And then she was fading away in the flames, and Armand tried to reach for her fingers, tried to grasp her for the one last chance to take her from the ship and its terrible fire, but then they were closing in around him, and with the final glance to where his mother had slipped away, Armand had jumped from the boards of the burning ship and into the water below.

"No pirates." He thought he had regained a grip on his calm, but the very name spoken to the room at large was enough to make his blood turn cold. "I will never grant any mercy to pirates, whatever their good intentions might be."

"If I might, sir..." Harrington spoke quietly. For all that he came across as a bumbling fool, the man had a certain amount of courage. Armand felt as though fire was shooting from his ears, and he was itching for a fight. "Catalina Sol is more of a mercenary type. Of what I've heard, she's never even killed a man who didn't rightly deserve it."

And Armand had thought he had a headache before. "I will work with a pirate," Armand said, gritting his teeth, "the day they build a ship capable of sailing to the moon." Harrington paled and stepped back. Armand rethought his earlier assessment.

"Now, if anyone else has any other ideas, I would be perfectly pleased to hear them. But under no circumstances, and I make this quite clear, *no* circumstances, will I ever enter a partnership with a pirate. I don't care who the pirate is, and I don't care what they do." Even Wendell looked as though he would much rather be battling mad dogs with his fists than stay in Armand's office a moment longer, but Armand didn't care. He was exhausted, worried, and frustrated, and these were his closest advisors. Surely, they would survive.

"Go," he said quietly, his mind whirling like a sail in heavy winds. He couldn't think. He didn't want to sit, but he didn't want to stand. His stomach protested, but he couldn't eat.

The three men didn't move.

"I said *go*," Armand shouted to them and felt a pang of guilt at the outburst. It wasn't their fault his brother had been kidnapped and was being held for the worst type of ransom to be found on the open market. "I'm sorry." They turned quickly. "I just need to think."

Harrington nodded for the three of them, and then Armand really was alone as the door clicked into place. He was alone in the room, alone in his house, the absence of his younger brother, the one he had sworn always to protect, more powerful with each passing moment. Had he been overly reactive to Spritz's suggestion? He didn't think so. No good at all would result from working with pirates. He'd be damned if he would leave another of his family members ever again at their mercy.

23

Chapter Three

He wasn't asleep, when the first cannon fired. Of course he wasn't. Sleeping was for men with clear minds and nothing to fear. Armand, with his brother kidnapped and a ransom demanded of his office and no thought or clue as to what to do next, did not sleep.

The single positive to be found in this unfortunate circumstance was, when the first cannon fired, hitting a large ship docked in the port, Armand was not safely in his bed and counting his blessings but rather pacing his study with all of the tension of a large jungle cat, coiled tight and ready to pounce.

He sprang to attention, the way a man does when he has spent his entire life out at sea, dealing with the sin of society—traders, rum runners, buccaneers. Before he knew it, he was out the door and down the hall, one arm already pulling on his coat, the other fastening an extra sword to the side of his belt.

Ever since the day his mother had perished at sea, Armand had prepared for a pirate raid. He practiced fencing and swordplay every day of the week and trained against masterful swordsmen who graced the small island. He trained with a pistol, he trained with a rapier, he trained with a dagger. Though hardly a violent sort by nature—not something one would know had they only seen his exchange earlier in the evening—Armand was a powerful weapon in his own right. He refused to lose another family member or anyone upon his island, for simply not being quick enough.

His feet pounded the wooden floors of the front hall, and then he was out the door and down the steps of his house, pushing his boots hard against the ground until the docks and large ships came into sight.

And what a sight it was. Two of the larger ships in the port were completely aflame, fire blazing up their masts and setting their sails alight. The decks were beginning to catch too, and despite himself, Armand could not help but notice the beauty of the fire, as though the docks had turned into some sort of pagan festival right before his eyes. But fire always brought with it memories of his mother's death, of the knowledge that he would never be good enough to save her. It made his heart clench and his feet seem to adhere themselves to the ground. Fire, fire was Armand's most hated enemy. It was his most disdained weakness.

The sound of screaming pulled him from these thoughts, and he realized that among the flames were several large men, now approaching the docks and the land and the innocent folk who had only just closed their market stands and brought home their wares.

Though his legs ached and his muscles burned from the powerful run he'd just taken from his home, Armand quickly threw himself into the fray, turning for the small hill that separated him from the docks, and half running and half sliding down, until he was naught but an oar's length away from where the thugs stood.

Behind him, Armand could hear soldiers, and he considered the good forethought somebody had had to call them, as he himself had not. He couldn't focus on that, however, because one of the larger pirates was approaching, and he had to prepare himself for a hand-to-hand battle that would have impressed the Vikings.

Armand was not a small man, not by any stretch of the imagination. But the man now approaching had the advantage of at least a head in height and was nearly as wide as he was tall.

"We're only sending a message," another man said, but the smoke and fire limited Armand's visibility and made the blood in his body run hot against the night. Then, through the roar of the flame, he heard the man say, "Try not to kill 'em. You remember what the captain told us." The man before him, whose expression was largely reminiscent of a rock, looked at Armand with hunger in his eyes, and it appeared to Armand that he was about to be the main course.

"Mad Dog," the anonymous voice called from the flame again. "Remember the plan." Mad Dog, for that was apparently his name, sulked and then picked himself up and wandered off to, by the sound of it, throw rocks through the windows of local shops.

Armand frowned. Something occurred to him, and he didn't like it one bit. In fact, the more he considered it, the more he felt inclined to race after the monster of a man and try and beat him to a pulp, just for an outlet of his excess energy. But though he was mad, he was hardly about to embark upon a suicide mission, which also included removing himself from the billowing plumes of smoke now encompassing the entire wharf upon which he stood. He climbed slowly back up to the top of the embankment, breathing deep, fresh air when he finally could, and looked out over the chaos.

That was what it was, truly. While he could see

several vignettes of swordplay and hand-to-hand combat, the main goal of the raiders appeared to Armand to be causing as much damage as was possible. What was it the man had said—to send a message?

Though the night air was warm, warmer still with the fire blazing upon the docks, Armand felt a sudden chill pass through him. The captain of the crew, from what he could surmise, was not with them. He obviously had no desire to get caught and likely didn't want his ship to be caught either. He didn't want to be followed into the open ocean. He just wanted to send a message.

Armand would be damned to hell, if he hadn't already gotten there, if the raid happening on his island right now actually turned out to be a random event. He was certain, increasingly so with every pained breath that he took, that these were the men who had kidnapped his brother—and they wanted to be damn sure that he knew it. Armand took one last deep breath and ran to help put out the fire.

****

He hadn't slept in more than two days. Ever since the missive regarding Henri's kidnapping had come in the dead of night, Armand had been running on a combination of shock and fear, and then to have a pirate raid to top the next evening off—well, he wasn't sure he would ever see a bed again. More likely than not, he wouldn't be able to sleep if he did.

The sun shone, bouncing off the stone square, and sending shards of bright light through the town. It made every scene of destruction, every burned beam and busted window, appear all the more devastatingly broken for the beauty of the day.

Men were coming and going. His advisors had been standing by his side all day. Wendell tended to the cleanup and repairs of the islands, with his soldiers in fine form helping to collect whatever could be salvaged. Spritz was handling Armand's judiciary duties as magistrate. All that needed taking care of for the trade company, Harrington had well under control. Armand was of the mind that it made a great deal of sense to surround yourself with those smarter than you. Then, at least, you could count on a job done well. Perhaps Wendell wasn't smarter, but he was a damn good soldier, and the island, up until the last two days, had rarely seen much trouble.

But now, townsfolk were coming up to him from every direction. Their houses had been burned, their market stalls torched, their bread and grain taken. He felt a deep sympathy for them, every hardworking sod who had been so close to making ends meet and had been forced to start all anew. Armand had always respected those who worked hard. Even when their family had been living in London, he had shied away from the folks who spent more time in their dressing rooms than they had in their offices or the House of Lords, and he'd only been a young man of seventeen when they had left the city for good.

He felt the sting of his brother's absence with every worry and complaint the people brought his way. Henri was good at this kind of work, reassuring folks that they would help them rebuild the town, helping those who had lost so much in the raid the night before. It occurred to Armand just how much he had to lose, if he didn't do *something* to get his brother back soon. He would lose his brother, the business, and the island, just so a single pirate crew could send him a message. He didn't think so. Not if hell froze around him.

Armand was deep in thought when Spritz approached him. Normally, the expression upon the older man's face was kind, if always a little reserved. But when he walked in his direction now, Armand felt the weight of an anchor drop into his stomach. What else could possibly go wrong? Armand's mind twisted over about how much they had already lost to this one band of pirates.

"Sir," Spritz said quietly, taking him off to the side and leaning his head toward Armand so he could whisper softly. "There has been a death."

Armand's heart went stone cold, as his first thought—that the pirates had disposed of his brother's body upon the island shores—came and went. They needed Henri for bartering, or at the very least, perceived bartering, and they were smart enough to know it. Still, someone's family was suffering for the tragedy—a tragedy he hadn't prevented.

"Who is it?" Armand asked, and even he could hear the steel edge to his voice. How had so much gone so wrong and so very quickly?

"A boy from the smithy's," Spritz said quickly. "His father is William Tomlinson."

Armand nodded, steeling his reserve so he might turn and go directly to visit the boy's father.

"I believe it was an accident, sir," Spritz added. "They think he might have perished in the fires."

Armand went to respond, but before he got the chance, there was a scream from the market. He and Spritz turned to face the noise and saw a woman, hunched over a form a little way from where they stood.

"My boy," she shrieked, giving no mind to the crowd that had gathered around her. "Jonathan!" She was wailing now, and as Armand began to walk toward her, he became more aware with every step that if he had simply heeded the ransom demands, this young boy would have lived to see another day.

"Mrs. Tomlinson," he said quietly. He turned to the man that was standing beside her, one arm on her shoulder, the rest of his body shaking with silent sobs. "Master Tomlinson." They acknowledged his presence as best they could and Armand continued, "I will make it my duty to find the men responsible for this, and they will be hanged." He paused, his own words seemingly stuck in his throat. "And I would like to have young Jonathan buried upon the estate grounds." It was only then that Jonathan's mother looked up to meet his eyes.

"Sir," she said, her eyes shining with unspoken questions.

"His death is a mark upon us all," Armand said, leaving out the full truth. The full truth was that the young boy with the dark hair and the long eyelashes, who looked as though he would wake at any moment, resembled Henri at a young age more than Armand would have thought possible. The truth was Armand felt a potent mixture of fear, relief, and guilt. The truth was, as he looked at the Tomlinsons, their horror still fresh, he knew what he had to do, and he was going to do it.

Armand turned back to Spritz, who had followed him to the boy's grieving parents.

"Fetch me Catalina Sol," he said.

Chapter Four

Catalina thought about it, her mind wandering so much that the boards of wood on the far wall began to move with the rise and crest of the sea. She thought about it, as she began to pace the room, her eyes roaming the great expansive darkness out the window. Oftentimes, Catalina was struck by the vastness of the ocean. It reminded her of her own place in the world, of how they all needed to do what they could to get by.

The moon struck the surface of the water, illuminating it in streaks of silvery white, and Catalina knew, without a doubt, what she needed to do. There was no use thinking about it any further.

She never got a name. If a person needed to find her, they found her. As was the case with the proposition she now considered. All she knew about the man for whom she would be working, if she decided that to be the way of things, was that he was a local magistrate, an earl, and the son of some island royal somewhere. Whether all the information she received was trustworthy or not, Catalina didn't know and she didn't care, as long as she had enough details to complete her mission. Men who roamed in her circles, both those who worked for her and those she worked for, had their own versions of the truth, and that was how she preferred it.

She wasn't going to condemn them. After all, no

one aboard the *Liberté* had ever heard the name Charlotte Talbot, and if she had anything to say about it, they never would.

She would take the meeting, of course, meet with the man and determine exactly what kind of work he needed done. They ran in strange circles, but Catalina had her limits, and she made it quite clear to her clientele exactly where she drew the line. When one was a sought-after, if not slightly feared, vagabond mercenary, rum trader, and all around notorious person, one could make demands that other people did their best to meet.

It would be the pragmatic choice, to take the job—a kidnapping of some sort or another, as was told by the flushed, sweaty-faced messenger who had stammered the information to her in the pub. She hadn't managed to get out of him exactly *who* had been kidnapped, but she'd learn that soon enough. It would be no skin off her back to meet the man. She was bound for Hispaniola in the first place, and she'd told the messenger to request his employer's presence at one of the dozens of anonymous pubs down the street in the bustling port town a few miles from Dwyer House. When you ran the ship, you made the rules.

There was a greater impetus to meet with the stranger, and Catalina knew it. Dwyer House. It was time to move forward with all that she and Antonia had discussed. She would buy a new house—expand her operations, save more of the wandering souls who floated her way, just as each of them saved her.

So why, if the whole matter made such damnable sense, was she even debating it? There should be no question at all as to what needed doing for the cause she had left everything behind for—her family, her home, the only country she had ever known. This mattered, Dwyer House mattered, and sacrifice came with the territory.

She pushed aside thoughts of home, of childhood and siblings and friends. The dream, more a vividly clear memory, had been lingering in the corners of her mind for days, and that made her cross. Eliza was safe at home. Armand and Henri were halfway across the world—well, maybe they were half a world away or maybe they were gone; she'd never know—from where they now sailed, but the sentiment remained. Charlotte Talbot was the name of a dead girl. She was gone, replaced by a woman who ruled the seas at her own discretion, who saved the lost and fought the evil.

Usually, that refrain helped Catalina through the lonely nights, when from the depths of her soul she longed for England, for the warm embrace of her sister, for an old friend. But now, when she needed those words to matter most, it felt as if they didn't matter at all.

****

The Dirty Hog lived up to its name. A solid inch of grease and mud lined the wooden floors, and Catalina could swear, with unflagging certainty, that the large walrus of a bartender who was now wiping down steins for ale had taken that rag to the privy with him. She didn't flinch. Seafaring pubs were not, on the whole, places for those with delicate constitutions.

She felt slightly better than she had upon the ship. When the melancholy came, as it would to even the most stalwart of seafarers on occasion, Catalina found her joy and light in seeing the smiling faces of her crew—young William, not so young anymore, and Rose McEwan, who would have been cast off to poverty, and not the welcome arms of Antonia, who was currently setting up fresh beds or milking one of their goats.

Yes, all it took to keep her mind clear and her resolve true was to see the smiling faces of her new family. Not so new, for it had been seven years since she'd set out on her own to make it in the world. They made it worth it to her, every sacrifice, every job they took.

Someone, perhaps two or three years past, had called her the Robin Hood of the sea, and Catalina threw the name over in her mind from time to time. They didn't steal, strictly speaking, but they took the money from those who could afford it, and they used it to help those who could not. In a sense of the phrase, they were a bit like Robin Hood's Merry Men.

Still, when it came to being a not-quite pirate, it served one well to remind folks that she never stole, never killed, never, except when strictly necessary, set fire to another man's ship. For years, Catalina had been walking a fine line of the law, and so far she'd been lucky as they came.

Perhaps that was behind the unerring, pattering thumps of her heart. She loathed having nerves before a meeting, especially when the feeling was such a foreign one. Catalina Sol was who she was, but it was also her *nom de guerre*, and when it came right down to it, she knew that she could behave in a way Lady Charlotte Talbot never would have dreamed. Having an alternate identity did keep her confidence in top form.

But she was meeting a magistrate. And not just a

plain old magistrate, but a man who, by the sound of things, boasted more titles than she did—not that a single soul this side of the Atlantic needed to know the truth of that. Until her dream about Eliza and Armand, Catalina hadn't even thought about Charlotte Talbot in some time.

She sucked down an ale, remembering belatedly about the dishrag, and grimaced. Well, if she were arrested and sentenced to hang for her pirate-like endeavors, she'd just have to figure out a plan. After all, she had been only eighteen when she'd slipped out of the house in the middle of the night and made a new life for herself on the open seas. She wasn't dead yet, now was she?

Catalina was so lost in her own musings, a rare occurrence for her, that she didn't notice when a man in a hood came into the tavern. Men and women often came and went anonymously through the doors of an island pub, no matter the time of day or time of year, and no one paid any mind to the hooded figure slipping in now and making for the far corner table, where Catalina had planned her meeting location.

In fact, Catalina's mind had been so preoccupied, it wasn't until the man, his large height behind the cloak blocking a significant amount of light, stood directly before her, that she realized she wasn't alone.

"Catalina Sol," he said, and though she couldn't see his face, she could tell he was looking down at the table, his visibility nearly as obscured by the hood as her own was of his face.

"You can remove your hood," she said quietly. "Nobody here will recognize you, and if they do, they won't care." The figure shook its head, and she shrugged. "All right then. Shall we go to the back room?" She was certain she would have seen an eyebrow rise, if she had been able to see any eyebrows.

"I can ensure your identity will remain a secret," she told him, feeling quite weary. "But I find it imperative to know the truth of the person for whom I will be working."

He followed her down a hallway, and Catalina called to the bartender that they'd be in a back room, a room she had used for such meetings many a time. Even after the door was locked, however, and the lights burned strongly in their holders—for it was a dark and wet day on the island, and the gray light that came in from the seashore was hardly enough to see by—the man did not remove his hood.

"Sir," she said strongly, "ma'am?"

The figure shook his head. "Sir," he replied.

Something about his voice made the hairs on the back of her neck stand up straight. The same way a scent could make her long for another time and place, so could a voice bring to mind a dalliance in a ballroom or a friendship in the bluebells. What Catalina was reminded of was such an absurd prospect, she pushed the thought away without hesitation.

"Sir," she repeated. "I will go no further in our discussions if you do not, at the very least, give me a name." The crew of the *Liberté* had come this far, and Catalina knew without doubt, efficiency was part of their success. Besides, she preferred to know who she was working for—it protected her crew from the hangman's noose.

"If you insist," the voice replied, and the same familiar feeling flitted up her neck. She wanted to swat it away, like an errant fly, but the sensation, the niggling power of a memory just out of sight, was unable to be pushed away a second time.

"I insist," she replied, beginning to feel irritated by the slow movement of the meeting. She reminded herself why she was doing it—for the widows and the women with children and the orphans. For the new house for them all. The thought softened her a bit.

And then his hood came down.

Chapter Five

Catalina had faced down more swords in her life than half the British Navy. She had fired pistols, fired cannon, swung by unraveling rope onto burning ships. She had dueled, fenced, boxed, and seen more than her fair share of shocking, violent, *maddening* events in her relatively short life. But nothing short of the literal end of days could have been cause for more surprise than what awaited her under the hood. For sheer lack of other response, she let out a scream that could far more easily have belonged to Charlotte Talbot than the mercenary captain of the *Liberté*.

"Armand!" Her voice—*was that her own voice?*—burned with shock and excitement and confusion and all manner of emotions she had long since left behind when earning her own ship and setting for the horizon.

His shock seemed as true as her own, and she surmised that he really hadn't been able to see much behind the veil of his cloak.

"Charlotte."

She wanted to nod. She wanted to do *something*, but she was frozen to the spot, her feet sinking into the floor and her body paralyzed.

"What the devil are you doing?" he asked. "And where the *hell* is Catalina Sol?"

She shook her head, finally able to get some movement into her frozen limbs.

"Armand," she whispered his name in shock. "I *am* Catalina Sol."

For a moment, the two of them simply stood, facing each other. Catalina took a deep breath, but it did little to steady the racing of her mind and the pounding of her heart against her ribs. It was as if she had seen a ghost, standing just before her in the flesh, as if her dear mama had risen from the grave and sung her a nighttime lullaby. For all she had heard, before taking to the seas, Armand and his family had perished in a fire set by pirates. She had never believed it, not really, but neither had she set about disproving it, either. Armand was a memory, a part of her past best left to the nurseries and schoolrooms of a London townhouse, to the fields and pastures of a countryside estate.

But the Armand who stood before her now—magistrate, she supposed—was not the boy she had waved goodbye to at the docks. With a bite of laughter that she nearly choked on, Catalina knew that her information had been shockingly accurate. This man did have far too many titles to his name. Good lot it seemed to be doing him now. No, this Armand was not a boy at all. He was a man, in the truest sense of the word. His skin was darker than she remembered, likely turned that golden brown by the brush of the sun, and his hair was longer with a silky thickness to it. He even had a small beard growing in, though Catalina got the distinct impression that he was not in the best of states at the moment, and that it was far more likely he was always clean shaven.

And by God, he was tall. His shoulders were wide, stretching that drab cloak, and he towered over her as if she were the size of a sea mite. For a fleeting second,

Catalina considered what could have been her husband all those years ago and allowed herself to feel the aching twinge of regret that came with the truth. But then she rallied, pulling herself together and staring him directly in the eye.

"What the devil are you doing here?" she asked him, her voice far calmer than she felt. Her insides were crashing like a great ocean storm against a weak hull, and Catalina knew if she didn't remove herself from his presence soon, she risked ruining everything she had worked so very hard for.

"I could ask you the same question," he growled. Ah, of course she had recognized his voice. There was no mistaking the hybrid of accents now, the French lilt to his gentleman's English, and the way he rolled his letters in imitation of his mother's native Indian tongue. Yes, it was a distinct combination, and it almost relieved Catalina to know that she had not fabricated it from her mind, when she had first heard him speak from under the hood.

"I'm working," she replied stiffly, desperately wanting for another mug of ale. Dirty dishrag or not, she could use the liquid courage right now.

"As a pirate." His words were seething, no less dangerous than a snake spitting poison. Catalina had heard that tone before, and she would hear it many times again, no doubt.

"Did you have a job for a nun, then?" she asked, deciding not to worry over the point of piracy. He would make the assumptions and waste both of their time, or they could simply move on with the business of the day, mainly, her leaving.

"I wish you had become a nun." He nearly growled

it, and a pang of guilt and sadness crashed over her. Truly, they had both faced many trials in the years since they had seen each other last. What was there to be fighting over now, in this impromptu reunion?

"I'm terribly sorry for having disappointed you, then," she replied. "The church was full." She could see the corner of his mouth tighten a fraction of an inch, and he very nearly smiled.

"The church was *full?*" he asked, as though he were making a concerted effort to keep a hold on his rage. Catalina pursed her lips and nodded.

"Overflowing with debutantes whose fiancés had left them"—she paused for emphasis—"presumably drowned at sea." She saw something flit across his face, and she knew she had lost him again. There was to be no humor in this meeting, hardly any nostalgia either. Too far from who they had been, she and Armand might never be able to reconcile their differences.

"We were attacked by pirates," he told her, his voice completely without emotion. "I nearly did." Catalina's heart dropped into her stomach. It had been so long since she had thought of Armand, and now that she imagined him nearly drowning, the idea of losing him was overwhelmingly sad. What the devil was the matter with her? She hadn't mourned over the loss of her old life in years. She wasn't going to start doing it now, and sure as God made green apples, she wasn't going to do it in front of him.

"I am sorry to hear that," she replied, keeping her voice steady. Then she paused for a moment and looked up at his face. She knew she should ask about his parents, about Henri. She should inquire as to what he had been passing the time with these years. She should.

41

Lady Charlotte Talbot, daughter of the Earl of Derby would have done so.

But she was no longer that woman, and associating with the man who represented that life more than any other was only going to drag her down. It would reveal her secret to the world. It would ruin everything. She would no longer be the woman she had worked so very hard to be.

"I can't help you," Catalina said finally, knowing that her resolve was weak. She was furious with him, for reasons she couldn't quite understand. Angry that he had never written, angry that he had never told her that he had survived, angry that he had surprised her in the land she considered so far away from her old life. Those reasons and so many more. Catalina knew if she didn't leave his presence soon, then all those reasons would disappear from sight, and she would go right back and help him anyway.

"Why not?" Armand asked, and she heard just a hint of a crack in his voice. It was unlike the boy she had known to be anything other than properly refined, properly polished and primped. If he were anything at all as she remembered, then this side of him, this nearly-begging-for-help version of Armand, meant that he was far beyond the end of his rope.

Catalina took a deep breath.

"I ran away, Armand," she said quietly, catching sight of those deep brown eyes. "I ran away, and I left the life you knew of me behind. If I involve myself with you now, there's no going back. I'll never be Catalina Sol again, and I very much like being Catalina Sol." She could see in his eyes that he didn't understand, so she continued. "It will come out one way or another that I know you, the earl you, the magistrate you, the prince you. And then what will happen? Who would want a mercenary who's really an escaped lady? People will start asking questions, and they'll find out the truth about me."

She went to turn, to leave because it was damned harder to say this to him than it should be, but he caught her arm and pulled her back toward him. He was warm and large, and his hand was a strange, wild comfort upon her skin. Catalina nearly balked. She didn't like the idea of anyone having to be a comfort to her.

"Please." The simplest word he could have said. Her eyes burned as she remembered growing up beside him, of all the dreams she had ever had of their future. But this could not work. She needed to get as far away from him as was possible, or she risked ruining everything. If word got out about her true identity, they would ship her back to England without so much as a *by your leave.*

So she yanked her arm away from him, though it pained her to do so, and Catalina Sol walked slowly toward the door, intent on not turning around to face him, intent on never setting eyes on him again, when Armand called out one last time.

"Charlotte," he said. The name stung like an icy blast. "They've got Henri."

Chapter Six

How could he have recognized her? This young woman, the one who had been first his playmate, then his schoolmate, and then his betrothed, was not the girl he had left behind on the London docks all those years ago. She didn't have little ringlets of curls to frame her face in some youthful style. She didn't wear the latest fashions designed for girls, full of lace and frills and brimming over with childish exuberance. No, this woman was as wild as the sea. One look at Charlotte—*Catalina*—and Armand's mind was awash with confusion, but he knew, unfailingly, that she would never go back to the hallowed halls of London ballrooms.

For one, her hair was loose. Wild curls framed her face, glinting in the low glow from the windows. She had so much hair, and it all flowed out in every direction, as though she were a lioness with a mane, dark caramel curls in the low light. For another thing, she wore breeches. On a lady of society, the daughter of an *earl*. And she was wearing *breeches.* There was no denying that those breeches fit her well, and Armand wondered if perhaps there should be a movement to put all young ladies of society in tight-fitting male attire. Perhaps too much sun had gone to his head. Here he was thinking about women's backsides, when his past had come back to haunt, and then reject him, in the

44

span of a single moment. What the hell was even going on?

He wanted to let her leave. If he represented the past she had left behind, she did likewise. The last time Armand had been in London, he'd been waving goodbye to the Talbot sisters from the deck of a ship. London wasn't his home. The English earldom wasn't him. The French title of *comte* wasn't him. He would have nothing to do with life on the continent, thank you very much.

But she couldn't leave, not without agreeing to help him first. He knew he probably looked a sight, for all that they hadn't set eyes on each other in nearly a decade, because of the sleepless nights and the turbulent days. They were quickly running out of time to get Henri back, and if he didn't do something— something drastic—more people were going to die. Perhaps that meant staring down his past, but if that was required for the safe return of his brother, Armand would do it without hesitation.

"Charlotte," he repeated, knowing he had caught her attention, hoping it would be enough. "They have Henri."

She froze. The whole room seemed to have frozen with his words, as though time had stopped, as though something larger than themselves seemed to hang in the balance. Finally, ever so slowly, she turned to face him.

The Charlotte Talbot he had known would never allow a silence in a conversation. She had been a young woman, not yet out of the schoolroom, but she had been bred to perfection—polite, refined, and even a bit overly conversational. This Charlotte—this *Catalina*— used the silence like a weapon.

"I will help you," she said finally, the words like the strike of an axe against a wooden log. "But under two conditions."

He hadn't come this far only to turn back now. Armand nodded, and she continued.

"One, you don't ask questions. Your titles, your holdings, your power—you have the ability to ruin a great many lives if you know too much."

Armand thought about that. He was a magistrate by choice, a business owner, and a man who had never embraced the titles of his youth. If she wanted him to keep his gavel at the shore, for Henri he would do it. He nodded.

Charlotte seemed pleased by this. "Two," she continued, "you need to understand something, right here in the room, and right now before me. I am not doing this for you."

The words sank like an anchor into the sea, and though Armand knew that he deserved every thread of anger that whispered over the steel resolve in her voice, they made him feel—*was that sadness?* It didn't matter. He'd turn the tides to get his brother back, though the woman before him seemed to be a greater challenge. He nodded and then put out his hand, as if this were a business deal of the most orthodox proceedings and not the maddest dream into which he had ever stumbled.

"It appears we have an accord."

Chapter Seven

27 April 1803
200 leagues off the coast of the Americas

The house was dark, but the familiar scent of baking bread led Catalina straight to the kitchens, where she discovered a handful of candles still lit and a fire still burning. Antonia was busying herself with the oven, and when she caught sight of Catalina, she took a surprised step backwards.

"Well, how's that for a greeting?" her dear friend said. "I could have sworn you to be a ghost, just then." Antonia had become the sister that Catalina had left behind. They were opposing in looks, Toni all dark where Catalina was light, her hair a thick swell of deep black, when she allowed it free from its tight plait. Catalina swore streaks of red scored the inky depths, but she rarely got the chance to prove it. Toni was tall, slender, beautiful, like a princess of some fairy forest, Catalina had often thought. No, they were not as alike in appearance as she and Eliza had been once upon a time, likely were still, though she would never know.

But in all else. While Catalina had a few years over her friend, their stories were similar enough to have come from the same chapter of the same book. A young debutante betrothed to a man she could never marry, escapes at sea in the dead of night. Antonia had found

47

Catalina, or rather, the other way around, when she stumbled into a sailor's tavern in the midst of a hurricane. That had been some five years ago now, and though they saw each other rarely—Antonia far more content with her feet firmly on the ground—they remained thick as thieves, a not untrue comparison on some days.

"That smells delicious," Catalina replied, in lieu of a response. She came around to meet her friend on the other side of a short stone wall and placed a chaste kiss upon her cheek. "I've missed you." Antonia gave her a smile, and then reluctantly handed her a freshly baked roll.

"You always know what to say so I'll part with my cooking," she replied, but her smile was genuine and mirrored Catalina's own.

"I've spent three weeks out on the open sea," she protested, biting into a piece of the bread and savoring its warm, honey-rich flavor. "Surviving on stale bread and dried meat is no way to live." At that, her friend arched an eyebrow, mischief in her eyes.

"Missing the hallowed halls of London, are we?" she teased, placing the bread down and taking a seat beside Catalina. "Do you recall how much food we ate? How much we didn't? So very much went to waste each night. Now that I know the value of a meal, it all seems so terrible." Catalina nodded. It was not the first time she had considered the element of greed and waste that went into an aristocratic estate. Now that she, along with Antonia, was responsible for maintaining the well-being of so many, it seemed such a waste that each meal had had seven or eight courses, many of which had gone untouched.

"I have news," she said, tearing her mind away from the halls of the Derby townhouse. She was missing Eliza. She would always miss Eliza. Antonia rested her head in her hands, a decidedly unladylike gesture, and nodded at Catalina to continue.

"We have a new job," Catalina said, careful to watch each of her words. Antonia knew enough of her life before landing in the Caribbean to know Armand and Henri. It would be prudent if she kept that information a secret, at least for the time being. "And it's a big one." Antonia eyes widened, and Catalina knew she was thinking of the cost of bed sheets and a new well and all that went into keeping some forty mouths fed and rested.

"Big enough for a new house." Catalina's smile widened. "We can do it, Toni," she said, using the nickname she had long ago forged for her friend. "We can take on more people. We can build."

Antonia's eyes widened. "Are you quite sure?" she asked, hesitation mingling with excitement. "There's so much to be done here." But her voice was tinkling with joy. "And who would watch this new house to make sure it all runs smoothly?"

Catalina shrugged. "You and I will find someone. And this job will bring more than enough funds to fix the roof and set up the gardens and fill our orchards." A few acres of fruit orchards stretched behind Dwyer House, but Catalina knew that another dozen or so trees would ease some of the pressure upon her friend's back. "I've brought you a new girl, Rose McEwan. She's nearly bursting with her babe, and she doesn't seem to hold her stomach all that well on the ship."

Antonia nodded, following her thought.

"We'll need a place to put the next Rose McEwan, Toni, and the next, and the next."

Antonia took her hand and squeezed tightly, her smile infectious. "You are a wonder. Truly, London's loss is the world's gain." She had a smile that could melt the frown off the face of Lucifer himself.

"I couldn't do it without you," Catalina whispered, grasping her hands in excitement. And it was the truth.

Chapter Eight

29 April 1803
200 leagues off the coast of the Americas

"Under no circumstances." She folded her arms across her chest and leveled a stare at Armand that could have halted the British Navy in its tracks. "You're not coming within twenty steps of my ship." Said ship was now lolling in the light afternoon breeze and listing slightly to the left. Catalina turned her stare toward two crewmen, who stood just at the end of the dock mooning at a buxom barmaid, and they scurried up the plank to adjust the sails.

"I'm not asking permission," Armand replied. He looked as though he was a fair bit more rested than when she had seen him last, but still the enduring expression of fear lingered behind his deep brown eyes. She didn't remember his gaze being quite so powerful or steady.

"It is *my ship*," Catalina nearly growled. "You would do well to ask some permission."

"You understand my meaning full and clear, Charlotte."

Her stare could have felled Medusa, and she was pleased to see him fumble.

"Catalina." He cocked his head to one side. "Lady Catalina?"

51

She ground her teeth together so tightly she was certain her jaw would snap. Here was a man who was far too accustomed to getting his own way, but she could simply not allow the commission to slip away.

"Captain Sol, if you please," she ground out. "And you're not coming with me. I told you—no questions." Armand's own expression was growing as frustrated as hers, and Catalina was beginning to feel exasperated.

"I'm not asking," he said, as if each of the words cost him. "I'm telling you. I'm coming upon this mission whether you accept me aboard your ship or not." She arched her eyebrow. If he were this unmanageable before they even embarked, how would he be upon the open seas?

"Are you planning to swim?" she asked, her voice humorless.

Armand shrugged, and she was, much to her dismay, struck by the sheer size of his shoulders as they filled out a sensible, perfectly tailored waistcoat. The man was one of propriety and standards, to be sure. Not another man half the world around would be caught with so many layers of clothing stretched across his body—not in heat such as this.

"If that's what it takes," he said, and she saw the note of honesty in his eyes so clearly it could have been written in ink. That, and an overwhelming frustration with their delay, snapped her resolve.

"Fine." Her voice was curt and every bit that of a captain preparing to set sail. "But everyone aboard my ship does their fair share. That will include you, *my lord*." Catalina said the words to goad him, and goad him they did. The vein at the edge of his temple pulsed with frustration, but she had the upper hand.

"Very well," he ground out, clearly a man unaccustomed to taking orders.

Catalina took a deep breath. This would be tricky territory to traverse. She had a ship full of stowaways, runaway brides, and orphans, and she was about to invite the island magistrate to join the fray. If they all made it out of this particular adventure unscathed, it would be nothing short of a miracle.

"Armand."

He turned, his face expressing the surprise he obviously felt at hearing his given name. "Yes, Captain?"

Oh, but that voice. When he wasn't being an irritating sod with his sense of his own importance clouding his vision, he truly had a lovely voice, all tinged with accents of the world, thick as honey and whispering of humor.

"Promise me you won't ask any questions." She must have appeared desperate, must have shown something in her expression, because he took one glance at her face, one quick look as she spoke, and nodded.

"I promise," he said.

****

Later that night

Armand had spent much of his life on ships. He had traversed the globe to visit the title he would inherit in India, if three cousins, one uncle, and a great grandfather passed away. He had traveled back and forth between England and France before troubles upon the continent—worsening from what he heard—began to make the trip a challenge. He had been living on an island for several years, a judge and a tradesman, *and*

53

oh, what would his father say about that? But Armand, for all his sea legs and all his stomach of steel, had never been able to sleep on a ship.

Oh, to be sure, he caught snatches of sleep, dozed in the afternoon or closed his eyes for an hour or so as the ship rocked through the night. But while the motion seemed to lull everyone else to the sweetness of rest, not unlike a baby in a cradle, it simply brought to Armand's mind the vastness of the sea, the swirling great ocean, that could ruin them all with the twist of a wave, with the turn of a storm. To sleep in a ship had come to feel like climbing into one's own coffin. With that had come envy for those who could rest, and so, instead of lying in a hammock and cursing the snoring men around him, he decided to make for the deck.

The air was warm, brushing his face the moment he cleared the top of the steps. It wasn't yet May, and an enormous moon hung low in the sky, but the Caribbean had never been a cool place to live. Even though the sun was nowhere to be found, Armand felt a drop of sweat slowly slip down the nape of his neck.

The truth was, he wanted to like ships. To him, they had once symbolized adventure and the great world outside of London ballrooms and French aristocracy. Even now, even as he had two titles in his name, and one title in waiting, all of which were being run by proxy, Armand hated the thought of returning to London or Paris or India. He liked upholding the law, enjoyed the challenges of trade, and felt free, away from the pomp and circumstance of the *ton.* It didn't much matter which country he was in—they were all the same in the end.

For a moment, Armand allowed his mind to

wander, thinking back to the days of his youth, when they had traversed the seas to return to his mother's lands. For a child, it had been a long journey, and though Henri had been confined to the lower decks with seasickness, Armand could recall spending his days on deck, watching the sailors and the horizon and the water, like a young man starved for adventure. His thoughts turned then, to the last time he had set sail from England, waving goodbye to the young girl, undeniably a woman now, who currently resided in her captain's chambers just below, doing goodness knew what. Once upon a time, Armand had known Charlotte Talbot. He had known her as the woman he was one day to wed, known her as his childhood friend and companion. She had laughed more, when they were young, but then again, didn't they all?

Still, he couldn't help but imagine what their lives might have been like, had they married. She was beautiful, no doubt. Striking and powerful and commanding. But would she have been those things, if she hadn't taken for the docks and the faraway line of the horizon? If they had both remained in London and done as their fathers had bid them, would either of them be the people they were now? Armand knew the answer before he had finished the question.

It was pleasant to fantasize about a normal life, if for a moment. Armand's life had never been normal, not since his mother had died and he had grown old enough to turn his back on the duties that lay for him upon her home shores. Everything was managed and taken care of, just not by him. Going home to India had never felt like home. The only place that ever had was the countryside estate and the London townhouse where he and Charlotte had played as children, chasing each other and their two, tag-along younger siblings. Charlotte had grown older, of course. She at fifteen and he at seventeen were no longer the children they had once been. Things would have changed, regardless of him leaving.

And yet, it burned in a way that Armand didn't quite understand, to find that their reunion was so fraught with hostility. He had been expecting a pirate, and he'd found himself one. It shouldn't matter that she was an old friend from a former life. She was a *pirate*, and that was the one thing Armand loathed more than any other in the world.

And yet.

And yet, she was such a beacon of hope for him. Henri had been gone near a week now, and to know that he was no longer solely responsible for bringing his brother home was comfort, indeed. As long as he had been a judge and successful tradesman, Armand had known he would never be truly safe. But they had taken his brother, and little else mattered until Henri was home and by his side.

A small sound jolted Armand from his jumbled thoughts of childhood and siblings. He had thought himself alone on the deck and tried to focus his eyes to see where the sound was coming from. Charlotte—Catalina, *now that was a difficult thing to remember*—had told him no questions. That had only made him more curious, not less.

The sound came again, followed by another, a different one. He hadn't much experience in the field of babies and comforting women, but he'd be damned if he didn't recognize the little squeal of infant lungs, as they protested something or other, likely the sway of the ship upon the tide. But surely, surely he was going mad, if he believed that he heard a baby onboard a ship headed out on a rescue effort. Short of Calypso herself rising up to join their madcap adventures, Armand could think of nothing more absurd than bringing an infant child on a ship headed for danger, if not complete disaster.

But this time, when the sound came, louder than before, Armand located a dark figure, standing in the shadows near the hull of the ship. She, for it was most definitely a she, moved slowly, bouncing the dark bundle in her arms and murmuring words that Armand couldn't hear from where he stood.

What the devil? Did this Catalina Sol have a single idea what was happening aboard her ship? She clearly had a stowaway from the port, someone who had no inkling of understanding just which ship they had boarded. Well, whoever stood in that dark corner, keeping themselves hidden from anyone who might be aboard the deck after dark, had picked a very poor choice for an escape ship, indeed.

He should approach her, Armand thought, but the idea was less than appealing. What in damnation did a man say to a stowaway woman with a baby, aboard a ship destined for a pirate stronghold on an ill-conceived rescue effort? For once, Armand found himself quite glad that he was not the man, or woman, responsible. The best course of action here was to find Catalina and have her make whatever decisions needed to be made to ensure this woman's safety, as they continued upon their mission.

So, with that thought in mind, Armand headed

back toward the stairs and set off for her chambers. He had never known a ship to be quiet, and in his life he'd spent a great deal of time between the snoring of sailors and the crashing of a wooden bow against the waves. But this ship, the *Liberté*, felt louder than most. It felt fuller than most too, though Armand thought that might be attributed to the extra hands needed for the rescue. As he walked the short hall to the captain's chamber, Armand got the distinct impression he was missing a fundamental element of the puzzle.

He knocked, and after a moment's pause, she called for him to enter. When he walked through the door into her chambers, Armand was struck dumb by the image that met him. Her unruly hair tumbled over her shoulders, clad only in a linen shirt, which seemed to caress her curves, the way no man's apparel ever should. The glow of several candles, tightly secured in their holders, lit her form. One hand gripped a quill, and the other had obviously stopped short in the act of tallying columns in a ledger book.

"Armand," she said far too sweetly, as if she had never been anything other than the debutante set for England's ballrooms.

"Captain," he replied, giving her a nod. "There's something going on aboard your ship that I believe you should know about."

She arched an eyebrow, as if more intrigued than surprised, and motioned for him to continue.

"I was above deck just a moment ago, and I saw a woman." He paused, expecting the words to hit the room with the ferocity of cannon fire. "She was holding a babe, no more than six months from the sound of it. I'm sorry to tell you, but I believe you've got a stowaway aboard your ship." Armand expected her blanch, to stand, to shout, to do any matter of things that an ordinary ship captain might do in similar circumstances. Ah, but Charlotte Talbot, turned Catalina Sol, was in no way an ordinary ship captain.

"Ah, yes," she said, a knowing smile playing upon her lips, far too knowing in Armand's opinion. The sensation of missing something important surged in his chest, not for the first time that evening. "That's just Mary. Poor wee Jon has difficulty sleeping aboard the ship some nights. She rocks him on the deck, seems to help."

Armand stared at her for a full moment without blinking. Was she mad? Was she as cracked as an egg to be tossed from the basket? There was no other explanation for what she had just said.

"Mary?" he asked slowly, his mind processing about as quickly as molasses in the cold. "You mean to say you know her?"

Catalina looked up from the ledgers she had returned to, and Armand couldn't help but notice the small smudge of ink that just brushed her cheek. It was such an insignificant detail, and yet, it so painfully reminded him of the girl he used to know. Who was this woman, and what the hell had she done with Charlotte Talbot?

"I thought I said no questions." When he didn't reply, she let out an exasperated sigh and nodded. "Yes, Armand, I know her. And I know William, the cabin boy—orphaned at the age of two. I know Rose McEwan, the woman we only just dropped on the island, eight months with child, father far off in the Americas. I know every one of the mothers, orphans,

59

and runaways that I keep in my employ."

He felt like a fish out of water, gulping air. Surely, surely this was not a common practice.

She looked as though she'd much rather return to her ledger, but instead she took a deep breath and said, "I take in those whom no one else will care for, Armand. I have a house upon the island, and a woman who oversees our charges. Some take up skills there; others I train to be fighters, if they'd like." She paused and looked at him, the challenge in her eyes unmistakable, as if to say, *go on, I dare you.* "The woman you saw above deck is named Mary Smyth. She's the second-best swordsman upon this ship, and she's been in my employ a year and three months. The babe turns one the end of the week."

His chest began to fill with a powerful rage, a mixture of confusion and anger, and Armand finally seemed able to locate his voice. "Are you telling me we're taking orphans and pregnant mothers to retrieve my brother?" he asked, trying to school his tone so as not to wake the rest of the ship. He had little doubt he could take on several of her best swordsmen, but there was no question of an undying loyalty to the captain, and Armand didn't feel up to facing a mob while on a ship and without an escape strategy.

"No." She said it with a force that took him aback. Surely, this young woman of the *ton* had learned a trick or two about dealing with powerful men through her years at sea. "I am telling you we are taking skilled warriors to battle, to retrieve your brother."

She paused for a moment, and Armand swore, for a flash of an eye, she looked tired, worn, a little weathered. He didn't like that he noticed that, not one bit.

"Armand, because I fled, avoiding a marriage to a man who likely would have beat me senseless each night of my life, my sister suffered on the marriage mart. Because you never returned, never even wrote, my fate was sealed by the first man who offered for my hand—for my dowry, to be exact. I refuse, upon my life and all that I own, to ever force another man, woman, or child to have to no choice. Do you understand?"

He didn't understand; Catalina could tell that from the moment she told him. He had no thought, no comprehension at all, as to why she might take in the needy and lost souls of a world with no use for them. After all, why should he have any sympathy? Here was a man with, if she recalled correctly, two or three titles to his name, upon the shores of as many individual countries, and he didn't attend to a single one of them. Here was a man who had never once suffered for his role in the world, had never once been forced to make a choice of two evils for his future. Flee or suffer? Run or die? She knew the story of each orphan, thief, and mother aboard her ship, and every single one pulled at the deep down heartstrings that reverberated with ever-increasing love for her new family.

"Is there anything more, my lord?" The title was intentional, and she saw the flicker of irritation as it spanned his golden-brown eyes. Damn the man, for all his finery and beauty. Underneath, he was just another lord—yet another gentleman with a title and lands and funds, who couldn't ever understand the troubles of Rose or Will or Mary. As she said it, however, Catalina knew their tentative hold on friendship, whatever might have come from once having anticipated a future together, was gone—snapped in two by the paths they had taken well before reconvening. Well, so be it. She had no mind to change her path. Things were working here—she had Dwyer House, potentially another on the way, and the friends and family she had taken in to care for. She didn't need him for anything more than the funds he provided. She wasn't on this mission for Armand anyway, but for his cheerful, lovable brother, Henri, who had a heart of gold and would likely not fare well in the hands of a pirate crew.

"No, captain," he sneered, and that hurt far more than it should have—a pinch in her chest that Catalina knew would be difficult to reconcile. "That's all." And then he was out the door, slamming it behind him.

Chapter Nine

Armand was feeling particularly irritable when the ship pulled into port upon a small island the following morning. In addition to going most of the night without sleep, he had spent several hours considering and reconsidering the words of his old friend turned pirate she-captain, words he had still not managed to comprehend, even as the sun rose over the glossy horizon and the crewmembers filed aboard the deck to join the late-night hands.

What the devil had she meant by blaming him for the way her sister had been treated upon the marriage mart in London? And what the devil was she doing with a ship full of runaways and vagabonds? She couldn't possibly run the system for long—where would the money come from? What if something happened to her?

He tried not to consider the possibility that something could happen to her. After all, Charlotte Talbot would have been a woman to worry about. Charlotte Talbot would have needed a parasol in the sun, and a chamber to herself below the deck. But this was a woman who could do more than manage on her own. This was a woman who made the rules and decisions that others followed. She didn't need his protection, and she most certainly didn't need his sympathy.

63

They finished docking the ship, and Catalina called to the crew, reminding them all to be back aboard by the time the sun was high in the sky. They were on an errand, and it wouldn't take long.

Catalina didn't give him permission to follow, but neither did she stop him, as she rounded a small turn and walked into a pub called the Squid and Swell. The floors were slick with ale, and the single room smelled only a shade better than a privy. He didn't want to trust her, but somewhere along the way, he had come to believe that Captain Catalina Sol did everything for a good reason.

"Attention, my good men," she said, walking through the door of the pub with all the fanfare of a jester preparing to take to the stage and all the confidence of a pirate seizing a ship. "If I might have all your attention, please." The room, despite the level of noise that had been emanating from drunken sailors and buccaneers only a moment before, fell to a pin-drop silence in an instant. For a moment, Armand allowed himself to be curious about her plan, but then he heard a man at the bar mumble to the person beside him.

"That's Catalina Sol, that is."

Armand's eyebrow nearly flew into his hair. Was her reputation so far reaching as to be able to quiet an entire tavern of vagabond men? The other man's response gave answer to Armand's internal question.

"I heard she killed ten men with a single pistol," the man replied, low and nervous. "And she did it without taking a shot." That, Armand had a difficult time believing, but even he could appreciate a good rumor when he heard one.

"My friends," Catalina was saying now, for all the

room like a politician in the British House of Lords, "we are looking for a man by the name of Henri de Bourbon, second son of Winston de Bourbon, and recently kidnapped."

Armand could hear the room's collective breath, as if anyone who interrupted her might doom them all. *Good God*, was this powerful force the same woman who had just told him about protecting the women and babies living on the edges of society?

"If you might happen to know of a man who has information on the young de Bourbon, I would be most pleased to hear it." She looked around the room, her gaze as powerful and potent as a sea preparing for storms. "As most of you are aware, I'm good for a handsome payout to the man with the information I seek."

This appeared to be the end of her small speech, and Armand followed her to the bar just across the room. As they settled into two stools and ordered large tankards of watery ale, Armand found he could no longer keep his curiosity hidden.

"What do we do now?" he asked her, looking around the room, as if expecting his brother to walk through the damned door at any moment, which was, of course, a fantasy. Catalina stared straight ahead and sipped at her drink.

"Now we wait," she said, a note of exhaustion slipping into her voice. "Oh, for God's sake, Armand, stop looking around."

He turned to her.

"Just be patient. You'll know if I need you."

He didn't like the thought of it, of not being needed, of allowing another person—hell, a lady of society—to be the one in charge of the dangerous decisions. But he knew he had to give in. He was not the man in charge right now. She was, and if he had any hope of retrieving Henri alive, he was damn well going to listen to what she had to say. It didn't matter if that thought pained him more than he could say.

As it turned out, Armand didn't need to wait very long for Catalina's efforts to bear fruit. They were sitting in silence, nursing their drinks, more for something to do than anything, when there was a resounding click behind them, a click Armand recognized all too well.

"Gentlemen." Catalina said it without turning around, and Armand could see out of the corner of his eye that two men were standing behind them now. One had a gun squarely tucked against her back, and his finger was cocking it, even as she spoke. "How kind of you to join us."

How the hell was her voice so calm? He was certain the whole pub could hear his heart pounding in his chest. He had been on the receiving end of a pistol's attentions and knew the feeling of wondering whether you might live to see another day all too well. That her voice was both steady, and even slightly arrogant, was a testament to her power as a fighter, Armand realized.

"Pity you were just leaving," the man with the gun said, his voice tinged with an Irish accent—that of the gruff, uneducated seaman.

"You must have mistaken me for someone who takes kindly to threats," Catalina said, and Armand could see a gleam in her eye from where he sat. It wasn't fear, however, but something else—excitement. Of course, she would be excited about being held at gunpoint. The rest of the day had been thrown so on its head, why would this be any different?

"And you seem to have mistaken us for men who snitch."

Armand could see her eyebrow rise, and for some reason, though he didn't know exactly how, he was certain that Catalina had these two hulking guards exactly where she wanted them. Instead of responding, however, instead of so much as muttering another word, Catalina flung her tankard of ale behind her in a motion so quick that it was over before Armand registered it. It had also caught the man holding the gun completely off guard, and he stumbled, just for a second, but it was enough time for Catalina to grasp his wrist with both hands and shove his hand backwards, until the gun aimed directly between the man's thighs.

The man was recovering from the ale to the face, which likely stung like the devil, when he realized exactly where Catalina had the gun in his hands pointing.

"I'll ask you again," she said, her voice all the more terrifying for its calmness, "do you think I'm a woman who takes kindly to threats?"

With their attention focused upon her, Armand took his opportunity to grab the other man's wrists, pinning them behind his back. Tied up and humiliated, they looked at her and shook their heads.

"Good answer," she said, her face devoid of all emotion. "Now, shall we have a chat?" She led the small caravan of four down the hall of the pub and into a room through the very last door. Her hand never left the gun, and the gun never left the man, but she didn't push and she didn't shove. Rather, she simply walked them in a line until they stood in the center of the room, the one with his hands tied, the other with a gun aimed somewhere very important.

"I'll ask just one time, because I am in a hurry," she began. Her voice was still powerful, steely, and strong, and Armand registered the thought that he never wanted to be on the receiving end of her anger. "Do either of you know the location of Henri de Bourbon?"

The men looked at each other. For all they both towered above her, their skin decorated with spider webs of tattoos, their faces fierce, they kowtowed in her presence.

"He'll kill us, he will," the first man said, his voice small and scared for the very first time since pointing a gun at her. "He'll kill us tomorrow, if he learns."

The other man, who had not yet spoken, took that as an opportunity to add, "He probably already knows."

Armand could see Catalina struggling not to roll her eyes. As a magistrate, he had been to a fair number of questionings, but this one was already shaping up to be the oddest by far.

"You came to me," she said. "You wish to leave the crew. Don't deny it. Just tell me your terms." The two men looked at each other, apprehension crossing both of their faces. Armand watched Catalina's face, and he felt a strange pang in his heart. Every moment he spent with this woman gave him more insight into the person his oldest friend had become. Not for the first time, he wondered how things would have been different, if they had both followed the paths laid out to them in their infancy. Yet, Armand knew that he would not have married the woman who stood beside him now, if she had stayed in London.

"I can provide protection," she said flatly, and Armand realized with a start that he was beginning to read her in a way the average stranger might not. One look at Catalina and there would have been no indication at all as to what was on her mind. Except that he was beginning to understand her small quirks and facial expressions. He tried not to think too much into it.

"I can keep you safe from your captain," she repeated. "Just give me the word."

There was no denying the piqued interest on the faces of the two men before them. Finally, one of them took a deep breath, exhaling it sharply.

"Might we come work for ye, ma'am?"

Armand started. Did this rough and ready pirate with lice in his beard and three of his front teeth missing actually just call her "ma'am"? A female captain and a woman with softness to her cheeks? Ma'am? Perhaps he had misjudged the situation. Perhaps she wasn't exactly what he had expected her to be. Ma'am was not a word lightly tossed around pirating circles, and there was never any respect paid to the women who took to a seafaring life. Catalina ruled the sea far more carefully than he had ever thought possible.

And yet, she didn't do so with force, Armand was beginning to realize. As a magistrate, he had the unhappy task of ensuring that violent offenders and thieves of the high seas saw their due behind bars or at the hangman's hand. But Catalina Sol, for all her appearance of a pirate, didn't even seem to have her own pistol at the ready. Armand disliked not knowing, disliked the softening of his feelings toward her, and so he pushed the thought away in favor of watching the scene before him.

"You'll have to prove yourselves worthy," she said, a slight arch to the eyebrow that could have only been handed down by generations of British aristocracy. "I need information." They looked pleased that this was all she needed.

"You're after a ship called the *Lilith*," one of the men whispered, as if even saying it might bring the good pirate captain forward. "A man by the name of Rodgering. He's who you're after—wants control of the whole trade route, he does. Thought he could convince the magistrate to call off his dogs if he stole the man's brother in the middle of the night." Armand could feel the rage in his veins begin to boil. Henri was the only family that he had left. How dare this man—

But before he got the chance to boil over, to give in to the anger that had been simmering below the surface these past days, Catalina cut in.

"Shall we make a deal, gentlemen?" she asked, and Armand felt his anger begin to simmer. It was likely the first time either of these men had ever been referred to as such in their lives. But despite himself, he grudgingly allowed her to continue doing what she appeared to do best. "You direct us to this *Lilith*, and the good Captain Rodgering, and we'll give you safe passage to wherever you would like to go. If you decide in the interim to maintain a position with our crew, I will pass judgment at the appropriate time as to whether that remains an option."

A look passed between the two men, as their meager understanding grew. Captain Sol drove a damned good bargain, Armand had to admit. The men before them thought they were getting the better side of the deal, whereas she had just convinced two pirates to give up their captain and location. Respect for her tactics grew, and Armand wondered if, perhaps, he had been a little too hasty in judging her role in the great game of seafaring. So she wasn't quite a soldier, in stead with the king and determined to keep his subjects safe. But she wasn't quite pirate either. The only weapon he had seen her use was the one that had already been turned against her back. She had only made use of her circumstances.

Armand didn't want that. He didn't want to have his feelings for the young captain change into anything, not respect, not understanding, certainly not a long-forgotten affection for a woman he was once destined to spend his life with.

And yet, as he watched her interact with the two men who could very well help bring Henri home, Armand was forced to admit that his feelings might just be changing anyway.

Chapter Ten

The ship was quiet—well, as quiet as a ship of some forty crewmembers and children ever got. But the deckhands were going about their job of making it through the night without incident, and Catalina had several men on watch, keeping a weather eye upon the two supposedly reformed pirates. She had considered, upon their first approach, whether or not she might have walked into a trap. But the men, for all that their information would prove invaluable, were not the sort of characters to whom trickery and deceit might have occurred. She'd be more likely to witness a man sailing his ship upon dry land, than those two attempting to pull the wool over her eyes.

All the same, she had set up two of her own strong crewmembers to keep a surreptitious watch, and with the knowledge that most of the ship was well on their way to a good night's rest, Catalina could breathe easily.

She couldn't seem to rest easily, however. In the days since Armand had first met her at the tavern, her dreams had been fraught with memories of home, of Eliza and their townhouse in London and their childhood bedchambers. She could remember the day she thought she had fallen in love with Armand, only to have his mother grow ill and the whole family leave for the far shores of India. Devil take it, until a fortnight earlier, she hadn't even known he was alive. He had stopped writing letters, stopped posting her small illustrations of where he had traveled and what they had seen. He would never know how important those letters had been to her, how strongly she had longed for the chance to see all those great beyonds herself.

Well, now Catalina had the whole world at the tip of her fingers. Now she could see all those islands and foreign lands with her own two eyes. Never again would her imagination be her sole companion in a stuffy ballroom in London. Next to marrying Armand, this had been what she had wanted most. It had been the reason she'd had no hesitation when the arrangement to marry a man twice her age pushed her to the midnight docks, aboard a ship called the *Sweet Lady*, and into the life of the sea-rough Captain Dwyer.

It seemed the sea had always been her calling. At the moment, however, as the dim golden glow of the candles danced across her dining table and the moon reflected through an open window, Catalina felt a calling to something else, something far more universal.

She was lonely.

The sensation should have evaporated with the arrival of her latest mission, to rescue Henri de Bourbon, the man who would have been her legal brother, had it all turned out as planned. She had always believed Eliza was half in love with Henri, even as her younger sister had scoffed at the very idea of marriage—only twelve years old when the earl and his family departed England forever. But Eliza was nigh on a million miles away, and Catalina had no one to speak to, no one to tell of her fears that perhaps she might never become the woman she expected of herself, perhaps she would roam the sea forever and wake one morning to find herself old and alone.

Being alone whilst older wasn't so much different than being alone at the ripe age of five and twenty.

For the need of something to do, she stood, pulled open the creaky doors of her wardrobe, and reached inside for a box. There had been three ships since the beginning, the *Sweet Lady*, the *Starling*, and the *Liberté*. But the box had come everywhere with her. The box had been her only tie to home, and the life she had lived once upon a time.

Damn Armand, this was all his fault. She hadn't even thought about what she had left behind in many months, hadn't thought past the next payment to Dwyer House, the next mission to afford food for the babes and clothes for their mothers. She had been busy, devoted and strong, out of necessity. Why now, with the arrival of her past, was it so easy to see each of those parts of herself begin to crumble under the simple gaze of a ghost? It wasn't Armand's fault, not really, but he reminded her of so many things that Catalina quite longed to forget.

She settled onto her bed and carefully opened the box. The small hinges creaked and hedged, until they offered her the contents—a stack of thick, folded letters dating back to before the day she had left home. For a moment, Catalina only stared. Long ago, the notes had lost any scent of Eliza or their home, traded from hand to hand along the seafaring post. But she could picture her dear sister in their London townhouse, scribing perfectly penned letters. Charlotte Talbot's handwriting had been a disaster of epic proportion, a truth that had sent several governesses running for the far hills.

Catalina Sol's was only marginally better, and entirely from necessity.

But Eliza's...Eliza had always been the proper daughter, the daughter that had never fallen in love or raced through the woods or gotten mud on her boots or run off to become a ship captain in the Spanish Main. It was all her fault that Eliza had been forced to marry a man their father's age, with only a few remaining whispers of hair and an overt case of gout. It had been Catalina's fault, Charlotte's fault, because who would have wanted to invite scandal through the front door in the form of a young woman whose sister had run off to avoid matrimony? Surely, it hardly set a pretty precedent.

But Eliza, for all her propriety and adherence to the rules, had never blamed her. She had been the most faithful of the family, after their father had refused to acknowledge his firstborn, after their extended relatives had cast a pall over her memory. Eliza had remained her dearest friend and most important confidante, no matter the distance.

Catalina was looking for Eliza's latest letter, if only to reread her dear sister's familiar words once again, when something quite other caught her eye.

This was an old letter. The corners were frayed, and the page was stiff, from having spent so many years folded up and kept in a box. Her newer missives didn't look like this, but the letter had grown pale and neglected. She pulled it toward herself, finding it suddenly imperative that she keep this letter close, that she read each line for the detail and memory it provided.

Charlie,

We've reached the Cape of Good Hope now. We're still more than two months from home, but Captain White believes it shall be smooth sailing. Not so for Henri, who has been seasick quite the whole of our journey. They say there is not much to do for his stomach. He merely must wait out the worst of it. I, on the other hand, am quite content to spend all my time on deck, watching the waves and the animals of the deep sea. It is humbling, for the son of so many titles, to be reminded of his own mortality. Out this far, were we to wreck, that would be the last of all of us.

Forgive me for being maudlin. I sincerely hope Mother's condition improves, although it shows little sign of doing so. I try to keep a happy front for my family, but we all know the truth of the matter. There is little hope of her return from the edge. Now, we simply must remain optimistic that we arrive at her home before the worst. At least that way she will survive to say goodbye.

Rather than thinking of that end, however, I spend much of my time observing the ships and ocean life. This is such a far way off from London or Paris, and though I have traveled the route before, I find it more interesting with each trip. Perhaps one day I will make a life for myself among these waves. Such is the burden of an older son, I suppose, that a future with that freedom remains only a dream. No matter where I go, Charlie, I hope you will visit. I miss you, and truly I could use a good laugh right about now. You always know what to say to make me smile.

Henri sends his regards to Eliza, and from all of us to your father. I wish I wrote with better tidings, but such is the way of things.

Regards,
Your friend, Armand Rajaram de Bourbon

Her hands began to tremble, and Catalina forced in several deep, long breaths before she was able to steady herself. How much time had passed in both of their lives since the day Armand had written her that letter? How many events had turned the tide of their futures, so their paths crossed again, but too colored by history to ever be as they once were? Images of all that could have been—a country estate filled with their children, an old age with rocking chairs by a roaring fire—flickered across her mind. He could have been a politician in the House of Lords. She could have done her charity work with all the clout of her own title and several of her husband's. The fantasy was darling. It was innocent. It was a lie.

The people they had become were built from their circumstances and their pasts. Had neither of them ever left London, would they even be the same selves they were now? Catalina doubted so.

And yet. And yet perhaps she owed him something, something for the past, for the future that might have been. The familiar scrawl of his handwriting, of his full legal name, his brother's name in dark ink across the parchment, sent a guilty streak flinging through the whole of her body. She had taken him on as a job for the sake of his brother, for the sake of the Williams and the Rose McEwans, who had likely borne her babe by now. She hadn't taken this job on for him, and she had been altogether up front about that stark truth.

But perhaps—Catalina was horrified to find that a single frustrated tear had slid down her cheek and was now staining the letter—perhaps she hadn't been fair to him. No, Armand was not the same man she had left behind, when trading in ball gowns for rapiers. He was not the same man who sailed from the docks of London all those years ago. But she was not the same either, for better or for worse, and perhaps, for the benefit of their families, for the benefit of their pasts, it was time she slackened the rope that held them both so taut. Circumstances had brought them both here. Circumstances could be damned.

****

"You're awake early."

It was a statement, not a question, but, though Armand kept his face toward the sea, he answered her unspoken query nonetheless.

"I can't sleep on ships," he said, and she heard the pang of annoyance creep through his voice at the admission. The gentry from London were the ones who should have suffered delicate constitutions upon the sea waves, she imagined Armand was thinking. He was a magistrate upon an island, a man required to sail regularly. Difficulty sleeping aboard a ship was not a minor inconvenience. It was practically a handicap.

"I remember," Catalina said slowly. She had been remembering a lot these days. "I also recall your difficulty sleeping in dark places, loud places, and drafty places." She saw the corners of his mouth curve slightly into a smile. Behind the mask of a face that had become this man's expression to the world at large, a sliver of her childhood betrothed still remained. Somewhere, deep down, she knew Armand retained a little of the young man she had once been so close to.

"You always did remember the important details,"

he replied, his voice not without a note of wistfulness, and another flash of guilt went straight to Catalina's gut. For all that she was roiling in the aftermath of her first life coming back to haunt her in the flesh, Armand was managing the same, in addition to the fear that his brother had been killed by pirates because he hadn't acted quickly enough. Surely, he could be forgiven, or at least excused, for his bad tempers.

"Share dinner with me this evening?" Catalina said, without preamble. "We're a week's sail from the pirate stronghold, and I think a civilized conversation could likely do us both a world of good." From where she stood at his side, she could see Armand's eyebrow quirk up.

"Feeling suddenly nostalgic?" he asked.

Another pang of guilt ricocheted around her hollow chest, though this time for her sister, and for the life she had left in England all those years ago. Even, Catalina supposed, for her father.

"I'm allowed." Her voice was defensive, as only the voice of someone who knows themselves to be in a losing fight can be.

"And yet, it sounds so much like a confession." His voice had taken on a drawling quality, and each word, each letter, was dipped in thick, molten steel—powerful and burning. She knew exactly what he was thinking about her trip into the past. But she straightened her spine and stared at the side of his face, strong, set, controlled.

"Priests and captains can both marry; why can't we both take confession?" she asked lightly, knowing exactly what he had meant by his statement and directly ignoring it.

79

Armand turned to face her, and there was something in his eyes that Catalina could not identify, a sadness, a knowledge of the sins of men, perhaps. Not his own sins. Armand did not have sins.

"I'll be at your cabin at eight." Curt and controlled. Very well. She had intentions to be tolerable, but there was no reason to have her neck snapped by a dark look.

"I'll be anticipating your arrival with my breath held."

The quirk of one eyebrow was the only indication he had understood her sardonic tone, and then he was gone, back down the ladder and out of sight.

Chapter Eleven

The problem with ships was, no matter how desperately you wished to avoid a person, there was really only so far to go. A man couldn't simply duck into a tavern, or lose himself at a card table for an evening. There was no disappearing to the countryside, or the inverse, staying in London far past the season's end. No, a ship, even one as large and decorous as the *Liberté*, had limited nooks and crannies in which to hide, and literally none that tickled Armand's fancy. He was a grown man, for God's sake. What the hell kind of man would it make him to hide out in a closet or, God forbid, a barrel, just to avoid her for a few more hours?

And yet, the thought of joining Captain Sol in her cabin for dinner had his blood pounding in his veins as strongly as the sea crashing against the shore. She was turning out different from what he had anticipated. Still a pirate, still a vigilante who not ought to be taking the law into her own hands, but a woman who clearly knew the rules of conduct when it came to seafaring and armed combat. It was almost difficult to picture her in a gown, her hair curled tightly to her head, almost impossible to remember Charlotte Talbot ever inhabiting her body, and yet…

There was no denying the expression in those deep eyes. It was subtle and easy to miss, but the truth of the matter was Armand was well versed in an expression like that. He saw it in the mirror every morning. She was lonely. It had barely occurred to him for a moment the sacrifices she might have made for the orphans and runaways for whom she now cared, but one look into those eyes, and Armand knew. Her sister. Her father. Her whole life in England—Charlotte Talbot would never be able to step foot back upon the land, for the sheer chaos it would cause among the stuffiest of the aristocracy.

But clearly she missed home, and the realization sent a pang of guilt to Armand's gut. Likely, his arrival had brought some well-buried memories to the surface, just as her arrival in his life had done.

Right now, that was all beside the point. He had managed most of the day without coming too close to the captain of the *Liberté*, but he was now standing before her cabin door, holding up his hand to the wood, where it hovered just above to knock. Was he absolutely mad to dine with her? She had a devilish wit, and a smile that could knock most men to their knees. But it was more than that. More, he was certain, than even their shared history. It was difficult to comprehend why, but Armand knew he couldn't deny his growing desire for Catalina. Her hips and delicious waist curved just perfectly for a man's hand—his hand. Her behind, in those completely ridiculous britches, was perfectly outlined and on stunning display. There were so many reasons he couldn't give in to that desire.

She was a pirate.

The thought steeled him, and this time, when Armand brought his hand to the door, he actually reached it.

"Come in," Catalina called, and he turned the

handle, walking into her chamber. Candles glowed around the room's edges, and for a moment, his eyes simply scanned, looking at the illustrations, the maps, the sculptures, until they came to rest upon her. He hadn't expected her to wear a gown, not this new Catalina. But she had changed her clothes, and skintight britches, made of velvet, clung to her body like a glove, illuminating her candlelit curves in delicate shadows. Her shirt, a soft white silk, spilled from her body in rolls of fabric, loose and flowing, but still providing a decent view of the slope of her neck and the curve of her cheek where it met her jaw.

"It feels terribly sinful to wear such soft material," Catalina said from her seat at the window. "And yet, every once in a while, it seems appropriate." He walked over to where she was sitting and looked out the window. Deep in the sky, the moon hung, its light doubled by the strength of its reflection upon the water's surface. There were certain things about life upon the ocean that Armand would never give up; the moon upon a clear night was one of them.

"You miss it, then?" he asked her, but they both knew it wasn't a question. Some part of each of them, long buried and only just brought to the surface by their serendipitous reunion, had always missed it.

When she spoke, her voice was not that of a captain, a savior, or even a sailor, but the wistful tone of a woman imagining how life might have been different, how everything might have been different.

"I could have married him," Catalina said quietly, almost so quietly that Armand was unable to hear, and he stepped closer to catch her words. "But for weeks, I tried to convince myself to be happy. For weeks, I imagined how my future might be." She looked up at him, her mouth a smile, but her eyes holding a sadness that Armand somehow knew no other person had seen in nearly a decade. "But the day before the wedding came, and I felt as though there was a noose closing in around my neck, and then before I knew it, I was out the door on a ship headed for the world at large."

Armand suppressed a laugh. He knew as well as anyone what it felt like to run away. But then her words begin to sink into his mind, and his heart pierced with a guilty sadness. He had left her. Of his own volition, perhaps not, but he hadn't returned either, and that weighed upon his shoulders. It had been his absence that had caused her to flee London and her family. There would never be a day when he didn't feel responsibility for that.

"Would you like a drink?" Catalina asked abruptly, and when she turned to face him, Armand could see the neckline of her thin, silk shirt was deep in the bodice, low and forgiving for anyone who dared a glance at her delicious curves. He shook himself, trying not to give in to the temptation of his own misplaced desire. She was beautiful, that much he could admit without pause. She was also absolutely the wrong woman with whom to dally.

"I'd love one," he told her, for want of something to do. Catalina nodded and walked across the room, pouring them both a generous glass of brandy from the decanter on the sideboard.

"What are you running from, Armand?" she asked him, and the way that her voice curled around his name made Armand's heart tighten. He hadn't heard his name spoken that way since he was a boy. It was bittersweet.

"What makes you think I'm running from something?" he asked her.

She sat in a large chair before the window, the many panes of glass giving them an unadulterated view of shimmering seas and brilliant, raw moonlight. Armand followed suit, sitting in the chair beside her, his face a carnival mask of moonbeams and dark shadows. In answer to his question, Catalina only raised an eyebrow, as if to say *don't lie to me.* Was he that obvious? Apparently.

"We never made it to India," he said quietly. Her drink had been halfway to her mouth, and she stopped midaction. "Our ship was boarded by pirates and set aflame. My mother refused to jump." His glass of brandy was suddenly fascinating, deep and gold, illuminated by the candlelight, and far less dangerous than the expression he knew was on her face right now. But Armand cleared his throat and continued, regardless. "She was very sick, as you might recall. With no land in sight, we had to swim for hours before another ship passed by. She didn't want to be a burden." Amazingly enough, his voice was steady and calm, and Armand felt a strange sense of relief at saying the story aloud. It had been several years since he'd thought much of that day, until his advisor had mentioned seeking out the mercenary. To tell the tale knowing it would elicit sympathy and not fear was a balm against his weathered heart.

"She made her choice to die with dignity," Catalina said. The words were true and honest, and Armand knew she had become a ship captain to the core. To die with dignity was the highest of honors. "She made her choice, not you." Catalina looked at him with eyes far too knowing and far too beautiful for a woman so hardened by the world. "I hope you haven't been blaming yourself for her death all these years, Armand."

He meant to lie, but there was no doubt in his mind that she would know in an instant. Instead, he let his silence be his admission.

The pause stretched into quietness, and Armand was forced to admit it was strangely comfortable, for all it swirled with memories and futures that could have been and the truth of what their futures were. Hell, he barely knew the woman sitting beside him, for all that they had spent their first fifteen years of life together.

"How?" he asked, almost sorry to break the silence. It felt nice to think one's own thoughts with company for once. She raised her brow, and Armand elaborated. "All this?" he said, motioning to the ship, and the direction of the crewmembers sleeping down the small hallway. "How did the belle of London society become the captain of the most infamous ship in the Spanish Main?"

She held her hand to her chest and smiled wildly, with all the truth of an actress upon the stage.

"You really think this is the most infamous ship in the whole Spanish Main?" she asked him, her voice pitched to perfection. "You flatter me, sir."

He rolled his eyes. Catalina had not lost every attribute of Charlotte Talbot, it appeared.

"And I was *not* the belle of the ball. If you recall, I was only fifteen when you left."

He blinked his memories into focus and nodded. "So you were." From the side, he could see her drain her glass in a single swallow. "Is my company so trying?" Armand asked, enjoying the dimples that spotted her cheeks when she smiled, small, but real.

"I haven't remembered in a long time, Armand. Forgive me."

He would. He would always forgive her, no matter her transgression. From the age of three, Charlotte Talbot had been his best friend. She'd been the one to make him laugh, the one to get him into trouble, the one to muddy his boots and tear his waistcoats. They'd had fun together, and for the eldest son meant to inherit at least one of three separate titles, *fun* was valued far higher than anything else.

So it didn't matter that he didn't know why she begged his forgiveness. It could have been her unladylike behavior, could have been her sharp tongue from their very first encounter, could have been the very fact that she had run from the life they could have led together, if only he'd been there. It didn't matter. Not when it came to Charlotte. Not even when it came to Catalina.

"You're avoiding my question." He didn't like how raw his emotions were, as they crept into his mind and through his veins. Perhaps it had been too long since he'd remembered as well. "How did you get here?"

"I'll tell if you tell," she said, that devilish twinkle in her eyes betraying none of the strength and control Armand knew she was built of.

"I've nothing to hide," he said. "But ladies first."

At that, she truly did laugh, and poured herself another glass of brandy from the decanter on the table between them. "No one has called me a lady in a long time."

So the wench enjoyed wearing britches and playing

vigilante sea captain. Why would that affect him? It should have no effect. None.

"Very well. I snuck aboard the *Sweet Lady* when I was eighteen years old, the day before my wedding. I spent four days in the hold of the ship, living only on the rations I had managed to bring along and trying to devise a plan to eventually make myself known to the crew. I knew I couldn't remain below deck for the whole trip. Hell, I didn't even know where the ship was headed."

He felt his stomach roil. What if something had happened to her during the time she lived below the deck? What if one of the crewmembers had mishandled her or treated her ill? Armand knew he would never be able to forgive himself for that. But Catalina was talking again, and he turned his attention back toward her.

"The captain found me," she said quietly. "Dwyer himself stumbled upon me huddling in a corner of the hull, hungry, tired, and scared."

Despite himself, Armand was enthralled. "What did he do?" he asked, trying to keep the excitement from his voice. Obviously, her story hadn't ended the way most tales of stowaway women on ships did.

She smiled nostalgically, and this smile was not fraught with the sadness of her other memories. "He offered me a choice. He said he would either throw me overboard, or I could earn my keep as a cabin boy."

Armand laughed. "That doesn't seem like much of a choice."

She shook her head. "He was testing me, wanted to see if I'd be any good as a crewmember. Women have certain skills men don't. Oftentimes, it's easier for us to climb into smaller places or tie different knots. He actually gave me a chance, and for that, I'll be forever in his debt." She drank deeply from her glass and took a breath.

"As it goes, I performed my duties. Did my job as cabin boy, then crewmember. Worked through all the chores and challenges that came my way. Before I knew it, two years had passed, and I'd become his second mate." She played with the large necklace that rested against her skin, drawing attention to the curves and shadows and valleys below.

"One night, Dwyer took me aside. He said that he knew it was my destiny to do more than man a ship. He said that one day he thought I could run one myself. Then he made me an offer."

At this Armand raised an eyebrow, but she quelled him with a single look.

"He said he had a trade shipment that would take two ships to sail, and would I like to captain the *Starling* on our trip from Boston to Hispaniola? In return, and if he felt I was ready, he could provide me with enough scratch to buy it."

"I take it you kept your dowry secret, then?"

Catalina shook her head.

"It's only since the death of my father and because of Eliza's kindness that I've had access to any of the funds from the estate. Whilst a second mate, I truly was penniless, working for my meal. It made me think about the poor, and the differences between us. Going to bed each night with dirty hands and tired muscles helped me to realize I never belonged as a lady in London. Coupled with the knowledge of what young girls are forced to do—wed strangers, live isolated lives, often

89

times much, much worse—well, it set me upon a path. We sailed to the islands, and when we returned, Dwyer held up his end of the deal, so I set about purchasing the ship."

Armand placed his glass down upon the table.

"You actually got crewmembers to agree to board a lady captain's vessel?" he asked, unable to keep the incredulity from his voice. "I must admit, I am impressed."

She poured them both another glass of brandy. "My first crewmembers were down and out sailors who couldn't find work. They wouldn't have batted an eye if I had been a gentleman captain who enjoyed wearing garters. They just wanted the work. That was how it all began. From there, I began taking in those who needed refuge. There are far too many orphans who run the beaches and port cities, and I offered them work. Those who had sailed taught anyone who came aboard how to help, and before long we were taking to the high seas, trading and shipping goods—the first traveling charity house, if you will."

He laughed at that, and through her smile, Catalina continued her story.

"Soon, I began to realize there were too many orphans to feed aboard the ship. There were too many women with children out of wedlock, who could not be expected to sail for many months. I knew I needed to make a change. Around that time, I met Antonia. She had run from the shores of Italy, just as I had done from my own engagement, and from there we developed a plan for Dwyer House, named for the man who gave me the chance to make it possible. And now here we are." She motioned the room around her, a hint of sarcasm peppering her movements.

"Your turn," she said, casting an eye upon Armand, which he was sure had been the reason behind her success as a fearless sea captain. "How did you end up the small-town magistrate of a rock in the middle of the ocean?"

He pursed his lips. Her question was no more personal than his, and yet, the answer required delving deeply into a past he thought he had all but locked up for good.

But damn it all to hell, he couldn't seem to say no to her, not this night, when everything seemed tinged with candlelight and spicy brandy and the ghosts of their past, for the first time in years. Perhaps it was her company, an old friend. Perhaps it was her smile. Perhaps it was best if he never thought about why he felt so comfortable around her ever again. Instead, Armand took a deep breath.

"So our ship was boarded by pirates. After the whole vessel had burned—and I tried not to watch it burn—" He could picture the day in his mind as if it were projected before him. He had tried so desperately to look away, but his mother…His throat seized just a fraction, and he took another deep breath. "Eventually we were rescued, but the trade ship was bound for the Americas and would only drop us at the next port, many, many miles from where we had been bound—Great Inagua."

She nodded, clearly recognizing the name.

"While there, my father grew very ill. He had never been the sort of man to hold high to the delicate situations, and my mother's illness, the pirates, the fire, her death, all became too much for him.

91

"We stayed upon the island for many weeks, sending note to my mother's family that we would not be arriving home. Henri thought it best if we made ourselves a more permanent fixture, as a way of showing optimism to our ailing father. For want of something to do, I began assisting the local magistrate's office in matters of security and strategy. Staying by my father's bedside as he withered before my eyes, so soon after my mother had passed, was not an activity I could countenance day in and day out. So I made myself known around the community, and when the old magistrate passed away, it was only natural that I take up his post. It was little different from my work helping to run the estate in London, and I liked that it kept me busy."

"And then your father died," she said quietly, her voice as sad as if she had lost both of her own parents in such a short time. Of course, Armand realized, she had practically been raised by his family, as well as her own. "You must have been devastated."

He didn't say anything for a moment, and then poured himself another drink.

"He never fully recovered from the loss of my mother," Armand said quietly, thinking back to those fateful weeks with a heavy heart. It had been far too long since he had remembered his parents properly, and he knew guilt still peppered his sorrow. "We watched him for months before he finally succumbed to the illness, but since arriving upon the island, he had never quite returned to himself."

She had curled herself upon the chair and was leaning against the arm. For a moment, Armand was reminded of a cat, one of the large jungle cats he had seen in his mother's home country. She was sweet and soft when it suited her, and dangerous and wildly powerful when the world called upon her to be.

The thought was far more frightening than it ought to have been.

"But you never returned home," she said. Armand stood from the chair, for something to do, something other than rehashing the past, other than catching her sad, knowing eyes, other than following the long lines of her thighs, as she curled into herself.

"I was a coward," he said fiercely, his voice filled with dark self-admonishment. "I didn't want the title, and I didn't want the responsibility. Staying on the island was comfortable, and for a little while, Henri and I simply bided our time, pretending to ourselves, and each other, that we would be returning home, to one of our homes, at some point in the future. There were heirs in India, but the matter of the estates in France and England were large and complex. I was seventeen. Henri was just thirteen."

He walked over to the bookshelf beside her desk and began absently looking at their spines, as he continued his story.

"We never left. The island became the place where we buried our father. Soon after, we placed a headstone for our mother as well. Day after day, we made excuses to remain there. The weather would turn. We wouldn't want to enter back into society so soon. I realize now my brother was hardly old enough to make those choices, and how much he relied upon me to do so properly. But I was barely more than a child myself, and I did what I thought was right at the time." Up until quite recently, Armand had still believed it to be right, had continued to enjoy his home in the islands, continued to run his estates by proxy. Every quarter he would receive the accounts of the two estates, but stewards ran them in his stead, and as such his responsibility was limited. Up until now, that felt right. It felt acceptable.

But Charlotte, *Catalina*, had reminded him of that life he had left behind, when he decided to hide away in the islands. He'd spent more of his life hiding from it, than ever actually living it.

Deep in the throes of self-admonishment, Armand noticed something from the corner of his eye. It was a folded letter lying upon the desk. The edges were frayed, and the parchment was nearly white, clearly kept in a dark place for a long time. No matter, he would recognize his own handwriting, even with as many years that had passed, from anywhere.

His eyes scanned the page, eventually turning to the date in the upper corner and Armand felt a wash of sadness through his whole self, followed by a remarkable and unwelcome stab of guilt.

"I never wrote again," he said after a moment. She had turned to look at him, and her eyes held a surprisingly innocent expression, one he hadn't seen in nearly ten long years.

"No," Catalina said. "You never wrote again." For some reason, the forgiveness in her voice was the most damning thing of all.

Chapter Twelve

Whatever demons they had been fighting in the other seemed to disappear below the surface, as they continued their journey to the cove where, according to their reformed pirates, Henri was being held. Their friendship truly had been forged the night before in her cabin, when they had spilled their pasts and their fears in stilted but honest conversation. It was nowhere near the friendship of their childhood, tentative and new as it was, but it was real and strong, and Catalina felt a fierce relief to manage that at all. Everything would change once they reached Henri, but knowing she and Armand had established a solid foundation on which to live their days, was a victory indeed.

Sometimes, she allowed her mind to wander, as the waves pulled them across the sea. What would it have been like to marry to the brooding man who stood at the bow most days and held a powerful command with such ease? Armand was a subtle force. Controlled and fierce, and undeniably handsome, with his dark stubble against his dark skin, gold-brown eyes reflecting like the corals of the ocean. He was tall and his shoulders were broad, and try as Catalina might, she had a devil of time keeping herself from staring at the sway of his back when he pitched in with the crew, the cresting of muscles as his arms bulged against his linen shirts.

She reasoned with herself that the attraction was

nothing stronger than a combustible mixture of nostalgia and loneliness. Recalling the days of their youth left her feeling safe and comfortable in his presence, and she was becoming increasingly aware of how she spent her nights—alone. If she had been kidnapped by pirate forces, her own dear sister wouldn't know of the event for many months to come. Catalina had no doubt her crew would make every effort to find her, but when the past comes throttling forcefully in your direction, it can be difficult to dodge.

Still, their friendship was amicable, almost easy. Though it remained a fragile sort of thing, she had little doubt of its truth. This wasn't the rekindling of an old relationship. This was the building of a brand-new one, made not from the children they had been in London, but the people they had become in the years since. Catalina was finding she rather liked this Armand. He was dry, sardonic, and witty, but truly brilliant. There was no doubt in her mind he would have run his estates like the best of them. Still, she knew equally as well he loved his work as both a magistrate and a trader— running rums, silks, and spices all across the world, not, incidentally, unlike herself, but without the army of orphans, thieves, and escaped brides.

They jested of their roles in the world, how neither of them had become what had been expected of them. They even managed a fleeting fantasy or two, about the world, had it been different, about what they might do in the future. Neither of them spoke of Henri, or what might await them ahead. Neither of them acknowledged that they had no future together. Aware as Catalina was of her own loneliness, she knew her crew and her families and her orphans would love and welcome her the moment she asked, before she even asked. If Armand lost his brother, after losing everyone else, he would truly be alone in the world. The thought tugged tightly upon her heart, and she buried it deep down, afraid of further analysis.

And so the days passed, with repartee and banter, with memories and jokes. They were careful to avoid exposing the truth of who she was, but by God, it felt good to remember Charlotte Talbot again. For all she had renounced the life of that lady of society, those had been eighteen years of her own story. To erase it entirely had always been an effort, and the very acknowledgement of whom she had once been felt like fresh water washing over her after a month at sea.

So, three days after their shared evening in her dining room, when the crew pulled out their pennywhistles and mandolins for a night of dancing upon calm seas, Catalina asked Armand if he would care to join her for a pint of ale at the festivities. She owed him that much, she had said. Just one pint. To her surprise, and likely to his own, he had agreed without pause, and they soon found themselves settled at one corner of the deck, watching the clinking mugs, as the crew began to grow rowdy around them.

"If you returned to London now, you could likely drink half the gentlemen under the table," Armand said to her, as they drew more ale into their mugs from a barrel by the mast.

Catalina raised an eyebrow, a small smile playing upon her lips. "Only half?" She hadn't been in society long before escaping into the night, but she seemed to recall ballrooms filled to the brim with drunken gentry.

He gave her an appraising look. "I have yet to

experience the extent of your skill," he told her with a grin that made Catalina's breath catch. Surely, it must be against some maritime agreement for a man to be so damnably good-looking, and so completely the wrong sort of man at the same time.

"Then I suppose I'll just have to show you," she said, turning her eyes on him. She had been told on more than one occasion that her eyes were transfixing. Why she wanted to transfix Armand, Catalina couldn't be sure. Perhaps she wanted to make him feel a modicum of what he seemed to be doing to her. That was the only rational explanation.

Truly, she had become a wild woman, in the years since leaving London. Once upon a time, a glass of champagne would have been enough to have her stumbling up to her chambers. Now, however, she could throw back pints of ale until the day that the sun rose in the west and set in the east.

Armand signaled for more ale, and they clinked their full mugs together. Catalina tried to suppress a laugh, but it came out anyway, a muffled, ridiculous sound between her half-closed lips.

"I thought you could hold your ale better than *that*," Armand said, one dark eyebrow sliding toward his sleek hair. Truly, if ever there were a man that was beautiful, in all senses of the word, it was him.

"I'm not drunk," she told him. "And I have no plans to be." The eyebrow rose still further. "It's just— well, I suppose I haven't had much fun in a while."

The expression in Armand's eyes was far too knowing, far too understanding, for Catalina's comfort. Instead, she busied herself looking over to the motley crew of musicians, now arranging for a small performance at the far end of the deck.

"I haven't either," Armand said, after a moment had passed, and there was a raw truth to his voice that stung Catalina down to the very soul she was sure she had forsaken a long time ago. "Had fun, that is."

At that, she looked at him. It was hard not to look at him, as his smooth voice, a little lower for the drink, curled around her mind, invaded her senses. This man could have been her husband. Well, perhaps not this version of him, but some variation.

"Have you ever considered going back?" she asked. It did seem as if all their conversations eventually returned to their first lives, but it had been so long since she'd spoken of it, that Catalina felt her past coming back to her in a rush whenever she was in Armand's presence.

"Of course." He said this in a tone so matter-of-fact it calmed her nerves in an instant. Whenever Catalina considered going home, it was usually a frazzled, tipsy thought, one that never seemed as clear or wise in the morning light of the next day. But Armand spoke as if he had considered each possibility, outlined every potential result, and decided to remain, rather than return. His rationality was soothing. "I suppose if I don't marry soon, those titles will eventually revert back to the crown." She gave him a small shrug.

"You're far more likely to die young out here," she said with a grin. "Perhaps you'll need to find yourself protection sooner than later." Armand drained his stein and shook his head, loose waves of dark hair rolling down his neck and curling near his jaw, his strong, powerful jaw. Beautiful indeed.

"No, thank you," he said, turning to the beer barrel.

"The world is better off without my efforts to procreate, I'll tell you that." It was Catalina's turn to raise an eyebrow. When she didn't speak, however, Armand simply took a deep sigh and continued. "I'm not the fatherly type, if you will. And most certainly not the husbandly kind either. No. I'm better off right where I am, no wife, no children, no estates to worry over." The words were perfectly even, not a hint of tone coloring even a single turn of syllable.

And yet. She heard the longing in his voice as clearly as if he'd written it in the sky. Armand had never been a good liar. As children, it had always been her forte to concoct the stories that would ease them out of trouble, if they came home with muddy boots or ripped clothing. But far more than that, Catalina recognized the tone, because she knew it in her heart. One day, he might change his mind, she thought, if only he could get out of his own way long enough.

"Would you listen to that?" Armand put his mug down, all traces of his earlier statement gone from his voice. There was a hint of childish amusement in his words now. "This is the last song we ever danced to, Charlie." The childhood nickname had obviously slipped from his mouth with his noticing, but Catalina noticed, and for a moment she was so struck by it, by hearing the name she hadn't heard in so, so many years, that she hardly registered the rest of what he had said. And then.

"What on earth are you talking about?" she asked him. "I was fifteen when you left for India, Armand. Still in the schoolroom. We never danced together to any song."

He raised his eyebrow again, a small smile playing

upon the corners of his lips. So she turned her mind to the musicians, listening to the song.

Something in Catalina's chest seized a little, almost as if her heart recognized the melody a breath before her mind. How could she possibly have forgotten that day in the ballroom? Surely, that should have been a memory that had stayed with her, and yet, much had changed in her life since then.

"Do you recall that afternoon now?" Armand asked. His smile was now of a different sort than before, friendly, less dangerous. "You were the worst sort of dancer imaginable, as far as my memory serves."

She laughed, a true, deep laugh that had her feeling heady and joyous. "I was the worst dancer London had ever seen!" Flashes of her dancing instructors' expressions crossed through her mind, usually including an elderly gentleman who had gone very red in the face. "Master Pingleton was distraught. He'd never had a failed debutante, and I was sure to spoil his record." Her voice softened, as she recalled the afternoon in which Armand had accidentally strolled into her dancing lesson in the ballroom at the Derby townhouse.

"I do believe that was the afternoon he resigned," Armand said, catching onto her memory. "And you were upset because your papa had promised you a new hat, if you were able to master at least one single dance." She nodded, remembering more clearly now.

"Of course! The new fashions had just come out, and I was desperate for one of the latest bonnets, the ones with the extra bows. And you stepped in and saved the day, as far as I remember." She gave him a grin, entirely to do with memories and not with ale. "My knight in shining—velvet, was it?"

He grimaced. "We all made our mistakes. I was only seventeen myself, if you recall."

Catalina did. Now that the dam had cracked, a flood of memories was coming through. She glanced over at the crew, who were playing a livelier version of "June Meadows" than that to which she and Armand had danced, all those years ago. A strike of madness shot through her, and Catalina stood up, holding out her hand to Armand.

"Let's dance," she said, the impropriety of it as delicious as a new spice upon her tongue. Never in her maddest dreams would she have entertained the possibility of asking a man for a dance, rather than waiting to be asked. But when was the last time she had been to any sort of affair where lords and ladies did that sort of thing, anyhow? It had been ages since she'd engaged in the proper etiquette for a lady befitting her rank, so why the sudden interest in the rules of propriety now?

Armand blinked at her for a moment, and he looked as though he might argue. She could see the expression cross his eyes, and Catalina knew she needed to stop the thought in its course.

"Come, Armand," she said quickly, still holding out her hand. "We could have been married by now." Both eyebrows rose into that silky hair, and she pursed her lips. "Please?"

It must have been the *please* that did it, because he was standing from the large wooden chest they had been sharing, with only a small stagger, and taking her hand. "Ask me properly," he told her, and Catalina couldn't keep the smile from forming upon her face, not that she would have tried.

"Lord de Bourbon," she said, with a rather unladylike grin, "would you do me the honor of sharing this dance?"

He nodded and bowed low, nearly so low that he brushed the floor, and then the two took hands and began the familiar rhythm of the country dance, down and around the salty planks of the deck. Several of the crewmembers paired off and joined in after a moment, and soon there was a makeshift dance floor right in the middle of the sea, full to the brim of stomping feet, as the country song took them around and through and over, again and again.

Catalina couldn't recall the last time she had enjoyed herself so very much. Her smile felt positively adhered to her face, and her feet—as horrid as they were at the actual steps—seemed to be moving of their own accord in a decent enough rhythm and speed to match the song. Her fingers entwined with Armand's, and while they would have, under any other circumstances, both been wearing gloves, Catalina enjoyed the feeling of Armand's strong fingers, his warm skin as it curved against her palm. For all that he was not a sailor, not a soldier, his hands were rough and calloused, setting unexpected contrast to the normally reserved man of proper decorum.

Then again, nothing seemed to be quite normal this night. Catalina found she was enjoying more than simply the man's fingers. Even at the safe distance they kept through the song, she could feel the heat of him, feel the strong muscles in his arms, see the pulse of his thighs against his tight britches. She'd bet a month's wage his thighs were thick with strong muscles as well.

A wildly inappropriate thought, but it seemed that the more time she spent in this man's presence, the more her inappropriate thoughts wandered. She could hardly keep herself from watching the swell of his bottom lip as it jutted just slightly from his mouth. A delicious lip, Catalina thought with some amusement. What would it be like to kiss that lip?

The thought should have been terrifying. After all, Armand was the man who, until just two weeks prior, had believed her to be the worst kind of villain, a pirate and a runaway. He was a league away from her, not better or worse, just so very different. And their past, colorful and strange as it was, made the matter a little more complicated and difficult to untangle. No, getting involved with Armand, in any sense of the word, was positively the worst idea she could have.

And yet, damn him, for the way his deep black hair glinted in the light that stretched across the deck from the lanterns. Damn him, for his sparkling eyes and knowing gaze that seemed to read far too accurately exactly what she never wanted another person to know. There was a draw about him, a need to be near Armand that Catalina simply couldn't explain.

And they were having fun. By God, it was the most fun that Catalina had enjoyed in ages. She was dancing like a fool on the deck of a pirate ship with the son of an earl, who had once upon time been her best friend. Surely, if stranger days had happened, none were coming to her mind.

The song came to its end, but the musicians didn't lay down their instruments. Instead, before she and Armand even had the chance to return to their seats, a quick waltz started up. Catalina could feel herself longing to move, to dance beside him for another song. Those deep eyes quirked in her direction, asking the unspoken question. Instead of speaking, she agreed by taking his hand again, and soon they were waltzing. This song, for all it was quickly paced, required them to close the gap between their bodies.

When was the last time she had been this close to a man, Catalina thought, overly aware of just how warm Armand felt against her. His fingers were deliciously curling over her hand, and for the first time in ages, in far, far too long, she felt as though she could relax, could allow someone else to share her burdens and her joys. He was a friend, both old and new, and what did it matter if he smelled like spice and brandy and sea air?

"You've grown much better at dancing," he whispered in her ear. His breath was hot and promising of something she couldn't identify, and Catalina suppressed a shudder. However attractive Armand was, with his thick locks and dark brown eyes, flecked with gold, she had resisted temptation before—she would resist it again.

"I've had several teachers since Master Pingleton left that afternoon," she said, rather amazed to hear a breathy tone to her voice. She was not a woman prone to that sort of behavior. If she had ever truly been a lady of society, Catalina Sol was not so now. The hand upon her waist seemed a bit stronger, a little more possessive as he spun her across the deck. Surely, it was her imagination that Armand was showing any signs of desire. He had no idea he was so close to her body now, she reasoned, no idea that his warm, muscled chest was pressing against her, making her long for something she had once expected never to feel. But in the light of a bright springtime moon against a background of music and frivolity, everything was tinged in sparkle and a little unreal, a little shiny and exciting and it made her believe in the sort of things she hadn't ever before.

"Who was your favorite?" he asked her, and Catalina focused her mind back to the moment, trying to peel herself away from the thought of exactly what was hidden behind his form-fitting britches, and not entirely hidden with their close proximity, either.

"My favorite?" she repeated, a small breathy sound escaping her mouth.

"Your favorite teacher," Armand said, and when he spoke, she let her eyes flutter closed, let the ripe sound of his voice, deep and rolling, like spoonfuls of honey, wash over her body.

And then, because she knew he wanted to hear it, because *it was the truth,* she whispered back, "You."

She hadn't been imagining his desire. In the next moment, Armand's mouth was coming down upon hers, taking her lips with his own and pressing her against the wall nearest to where they had just been dancing. They slipped into the shadows of the hallway leading away from the open deck, hiding their desires in whispers and darkness. There was no question in Catalina's mind of stopping the kiss. She couldn't stop it if the regent himself had walked through the door. Instead, she sank into his mouth, sank into him, allowing the strong, powerful arms of the local magistrate to envelop her, hold her tightly, as he plundered her mouth, eliciting small, breathy moans from the back of her throat.

"Catalina," he growled into her ear, nipping at the

path of skin that led from the lobe down her neck. He was making it damned hard to concentrate when he did that, and her breasts tingled, her mouth wanted, as he continued his ministrations. "God, we should stop."

Her eyes were falling back, her lids fluttering half closed, as he continued his delicious kisses down her neck. She shook her head languidly, finding it difficult to locate her voice. "I don't want to stop," she said, because if they did she felt as though she might simply explode, so tightly strung was her body, so deliciously anticipating his next kiss.

Armand nodded, and she could see the fire in his dark gaze, knowing it mirrored her own. How delicious it felt to be *wanted* and by a man with the dark beauty of tales of old. He was a knight, a warrior, powerful, commanding, and needy for *her*.

So she took his hand, half-pulling, half-pushing him down the hallway until they came to the door of her chamber. She couldn't help but touch him on their short walk, running her fingers up the length of his arm, feeling his strong muscles, as he held her waist, keeping her tight to his side. Had he always been so large, so imposing a figure as he was now? In the mystery and excitement of the moment, Catalina felt as though Armand had grown larger, all bulk and muscle, hidden below his proper refined exterior.

But then she wasn't thinking much of anything anymore because she unlocked the door and opened it to the room. Then Armand pushed her up against the wall in one swoop and slammed the door shut behind them.

Chapter Thirteen

"Do you know how beautiful you are?" Armand asked, his hand running down the curve of her cheek, cupping her chin steady. "Do you know how difficult it is to watch you wear those britches every day, and not run my hands over the curves of your hips, your arse?" His hands were doing just that right now, cupping each buttock and squeezing lightly. Catalina let out a surprised gasp, and Armand took it as the chance to kiss her again, invading her mouth with his tongue as their kiss deepened. If his hands simply holding her backside had this kind of effect, what would he do to her once they were naked upon the bed?

"I'm sorry for the inconvenience," she managed to whisper against his mouth. "I hope I haven't caused any lasting damage." There was only a hint of sarcasm to her voice.

Armand pinched her rear, and she squirmed. "Wench," he whispered, and the filthy word upon his tongue sent a pool of heat to the space between her thighs, an unfamiliar but not unwelcome sensation. "Do you feel that?"

He throbbed against her, and Catalina gasped. It was hard and hot pressed against her belly, and part of her longed to reach out her fingers and stroke him through the taut fabric.

"That's what you do to me, Catalina."

He was tracing a line of kisses from her neck down to her collarbone, each one punctuated by a sharp bite. The small pain should have sobered her, but instead it sent her rushing headfirst deeper into her mad fog of desire.

So, this time when he pressed against her, she did reach out, allowing her fingers to skim the side of his throbbing hardness. It was a light touch, tentative, but Armand sucked in a deep breath and nearly growled.

"You'll be the end of me," he said.

She rather liked holding that sort of power over him, and so she did it again, a little more confidently this time, stroking the thick organ between her fingers and marveling at its response to her. Armand obviously didn't like her to have too much control. His mouth moved from her collarbone to the sloping swell between her breasts, kissing each mound, until he was pulling her linen shirt down, exposing the very tip of one nipple to the room. She felt a wash of cool air, but it was instantly replaced by his fingers, which took her peaked nipple and squeezed gently.

She bucked against him, feeling his hardness meet the soft space between her legs. Even behind the fabric he seemed large, too large. Surely he wouldn't fit there, in that space which so seemed to be craving him. Catalina was fairly sure she wanted to find out for herself.

Just before she could ask, perhaps even beg, Armand's mouth was coming down upon her nipple and sucking it between his lips. One hand flew to his hair, and the other stroked more desperately upon his hardness, pulling and pressing back into the organ as if everything depended upon it. Armand groaned, and after a moment, he pulled his mouth from her breast.

"I need you," he growled, and the tone of his voice sent a pure thrill of pleasure down her body. He made her feel like a different woman, when he spoke like that.

"Then have me," she said, her voice as equally colored with desire. Armand picked her up from the ground and carried her over to the large bed in the middle of the room. Instinctively, Catalina wrapped her legs around his waist, pressing his hardness deeper toward where she most longed for his touch. She had never known she could feel this way. Surely the women had spoken of it, but this...this was pure, maddening bliss.

He pulled off her boots, and they landed upon the floor with a dull *thud.* Then his hands worked the buttons of her britches. The fabric had been perfectly tailored to fit her body, and for a moment, Armand struggled to pull them down, but then those, too, fell to the ground.

She was quite sure she made a sight to see, the moonlight casting a bright glow over her chamber, over her body, clad only in a large linen shirt and her garters and stockings. What would the *ton* say of her now?

That didn't matter. What mattered was the way Armand looked at her, as if she were a cherry tart straight from the kitchens. His gaze was deep and intense, and it made her breasts tingle with anticipation.

"Now that you have me, *my lord,*" she said, quite deliberately, "what are you going to do with me?"

Armand nearly tore at her shirt, tossing it off to the side, and then he stood, keeping his eyes upon her as he slowly began to remove his own clothes, one piece at a time.

The boots came off, then the jacket. Even behind the fabric of his shirt, Catalina could see the swell and sway of his powerful body. And then his shirt was gone as well, and his dark skin shone, rippled with muscles that stretched from his chest to the hills and valleys of his arms. His hands were on his britches now. Her mouth went dry, and she watched intently, as he slowly, deliberately, pulled the last garment from his body and moved toward her on the bed. He was large, so much larger than she had thought he would be, when feeling him through the fabric. His member jutted from a nest of dark curls, long and thick, throbbing. There was a small drop of liquid at the very end of the slightly red tip, and she found herself licking her lips.

Armand's actions bore all the grace of a jungle cat approaching its prey. As he stood over her, Catalina felt her heart race and her blood run hot, and she knew she was most definitely about to be devoured.

One of his hands cupped her breast, the rough pad of his thumb rolling over her peaked nipple.

"You're so ripe," he growled, his body throbbing in agreement. "I want to taste you." And then he was, just as before, pressing his mouth to her straining nipple, taking it between his lips and rolling his tongue over the bud. But then his hand was tracing the side of her hip, of her leg, rolling over the valleys and plains of her body and slipping between her thighs. For a moment, he simply traced around her heat, causing her to buck and arch against him. But he kept her in place with one steady hand, and the other one roamed, exploring the length of her thighs, the curve of her backside.

Then his fingers were upon her, upon the needy little trigger just above her entrance that had been throbbing and wanting for pressure of some kind, any kind. When he finally swept his finger across her, Catalina felt a great relief, as a wave of pleasure rose. Still, she wanted something, needed something more, something greater than just his finger upon her, just his mouth teasing her breast wildly. She wanted to be filled. She wanted him.

"Armand," she said, her voice the husky tone of a woman just before the edge. "*Please.*"

He groaned. "What do you want, Catalina? Tell me."

At first, she couldn't seem to find her voice, but the fire in her body burned and she was desperate for relief. "Touch me." She demanded it.

His hand cupped her breast. "Here?" he asked, and she nodded.

"More." Her voice was barely above a whisper now, but husky and demanding. "I need… more."

His self-control seemed to be waning, because his fingers were curving back around her behind and toward the heat between her legs.

"Here, Catalina?" he asked in his rough tone. "Is this where you want me to touch you?"

She whimpered in reply, and he slowly spread her knees apart, baring her to the room, to *him.*

And then, before she even realized, he had one rough finger at her entrance, slowly pressing inside. She sighed with relief, but her body bucked against him, desperate for more, for *something*. Another finger joined the first, and Catalina damned it all to hell, taking from him as he explored her body. She could feel her desire, slick against the inside of her thighs, as Armand slowly pulled his fingers out and slid them back in.

"I want you." This from him, a demand.

And then he was there, on his knees before her upon the bed, stroking himself. For a moment, she was mesmerized by the motion of his hand moving up and down his length, tugging slightly, but then he was sliding before her, slipping himself right into the entrance of her body, barely a fraction of an inch.

"Tell me, Catalina," he whispered. And she did.

"Take me."

He slid into her body, and the rush of pleasure she had been feeling turned into a burning, shooting pain. He froze instantly, and she could see the expression upon his face, concern, worry, *fear.*

"I had thought…" He paused, sobriety reentering his voice. "You didn't tell me."

She shook her head. The very worst of the pain seemed to be ebbing, in truth, and a small burst of pleasure was filling in its wake. "I'm fine," she whispered, stroking the muscled length of his arm. "Perhaps, just a bit slowly."

He nodded, sliding himself from her with care, and then slowly, deliberately, moving back into her body. This time, she felt very little of the burning, far overpowered by the heady rush of pleasure afforded by his delicious movements. One hand was still cupping her breast, and he was licking it again, all while slowly, carefully, sliding in and out of her.

Seemingly without thinking, Catalina wrapped her legs around his waist, pulling him deeper into her. It barely hurt at all now, with the way he was pressing against her, both inside and out, filling her completely, making her crazed for the feel of him. She groaned against his ear, and he took her mouth, plundering it with his tongue.

"You can move faster," she whispered. "Please move faster."

He chuckled at the desperate tone in her voice, and then he was moving faster, groaning as he filled her all the way, and she was groaning too, because the pleasure was growing now, bigger and impossible to contain. Surely, surely this was too much for her body.

And then he slipped his hand between her legs, rolling the tight nub between his fingers, and that *was* too much for her body, because Catalina screamed, a full-fledged scream, and fell right over the crest of her pleasure, waves upon waves of deep lust pouring over her, like swaths of velvet. She shook against him, feeling the throb of his member deep inside her, and then she finally, finally, came down.

He was looking at her with such a lustful expression in his gaze, Catalina felt her body heat up all over again.

"You're exquisite," he groaned. "My God." And then he was thrusting with far less control, his hand cupping her behind, squeezing, rounding. He pulled her toward him, shifting them both up slightly, pressing his hard, hot cock even deeper into her body, and Catalina knew she wouldn't last long, not this time, not with the powerful, lingering release she had just experienced.

"Finish with me," Armand demanded gruffly in her ear. "Please, Catalina."

She gripped his shoulders tightly, and then she was riding him instead of the other way around, taking from his body, pulsing and pumping, against the hard rod within her. And she felt him seize, felt her own body reach that pivotal point, and they were meeting thrust for thrust for thrust against each other, clinging tightly, desperately to the other, until she heard Armand roar, a sound which broke her control, and they pulsed into each other's needy bodies. She felt her powerful release catch her from behind, pushing her right past the threshold of control, and she tumbled, headfirst into a distant brightness, delicious lights popping before her eyes.

She distantly registered Armand sliding away, felt the heat of his release across her stomach, felt the weight of him, as he slid beside her on the bed, both of them breathing deeply, her heart pounding in her chest.

He carefully wiped her body clean, then tossed the rag to the side without a word. Then Armand Rajaram de Bourbon, magistrate, earl, childhood friend, gathered Catalina Sol, pirate mercenary, into his arms, and they drifted off to sleep.

Chapter Fourteen

Armand woke early the next morning, as streams of brand new light began to sift lazily in through the window. He kept his eyes closed against the sun, overly aware of the breaking pulse against his temple. He rarely overindulged in spirits of any kind, but ale had a particularly nasty effect upon his head, and his mouth felt parched, as though it had been stuffed with wool.

For a moment, that was all he seemed able to focus upon, but after several deep, even breaths, he cracked his eyes open enough to see if there might be a pitcher of water with which to wash his face, before going to fetch some breakfast. When he made to move, however, he felt a soft tug upon his arm, keeping him pinned to his place in the bed.

Cracking his eyes slightly wider, Armand realized with a horrible, sinking feeling, that his headache and potential for morning nausea were not the worst of last night's decisions. For a moment, he simply allowed himself to look at her. Long tendrils of hair spun out around her head, as if she were some mythical sea queen. Her face, normally reserved, normally stoic against the world, was softly curved as she slept. Those delicious lips, still swollen from their kisses the night before, were slightly parted, and she was breathing softly, which gave a slight swell to the deep curves of her bosom and belly as she inhaled. One nipple was just within reach of his fingers, and Armand had to curl his hand tightly to avoid reaching out to touch her. Despite the roiling sensation pounding in his skull, the lower parts of his anatomy were far too aware of the magnificent, powerful woman sleeping entirely nude beside him.

He blinked as the reality of his actions settled against his muddled brain. *What the hell had he done?* Images of their coupling stirred his body to even further attention, filling her, claiming her. He *had* claimed her. He was reminded of the secret she had kept from him the night before. She had been a virgin. He had taken that from her, caused her pain, ensured difficulty, should she ever choose to marry. She would never return to London society again. Not unless he did something drastic.

That she had made no indications of wanting to return was far less important than the aching sensation in his stomach that had nothing to do with his drinking and everything to do with his guilt. Armand swallowed deeply. Another drink would undoubtedly upset the contents of his stomach, otherwise he would have craved a glass of something strong. As it was, he couldn't afford the luxury, and his head reeled at that moment, as if to prove the point. Besides, the sun had yet to fully rise. Gentlemen didn't drink spirits before the dawn.

They also didn't deflower ladies, he thought with a pang of self-admonishment. Was he the worst sort of man? By God, Captain Catalina Sol was bringing out a whole new side of him. Well, he certainly wasn't going to go about righting the situation wearing only what his mother had given him. Slowly, carefully, he extricated himself from the soft curve of her arm, sliding from the bed, determined to keep the contents of his stomach exactly where they were.

He pulled on his britches and boots, then threw his shirt over his head, not bothering to tuck it in below the waist. He was on a ship of mercenary pirates, surely they had seen uglier sites than a worse-for-drink nobleman with a guilty conscience. So Armand walked down to the galley, righting himself against a doorframe before brewing some bitter coffee and taking a few pieces of toast from a stack on the table. If he had learned anything over the years of selling rum, he knew that soaking up the poison was one of the only effective methods of curing the aftereffects of a night's drinking.

Breakfast in hand, he made his way back to the captain's chamber. Catalina was still asleep. She had turned upon her side, and the long curve of her body caught streams of the increasing sunlight. He considered shutting the blinds for the sake of his temples, but the image she made against the bed was too tempting to say goodbye to just yet. Instead, he forced down a cup of coffee and a few pieces of toast. They were dry as the desert, but the roiling waves in his stomach seemed to calm a little, so he started upon another piece.

Across the room, Catalina began to stir, and he stiffened. Armand knew he had a duty. He may have forsaken his estates, left to be run by proxy in his absence. He may have forsaken all of England and France, not to speak of his mother's lands. But he had not forsaken his gentlemanly upbringing entirely, and he knew within his heart, down to the very tips of his slightly swollen fingers—he was never touching ale again—what he needed to do.

"Coffee?" he asked.

Her eyes were sleepy, and there was an ephemeral glow about her, with that halo of hair and the lovely golden color of her skin, from a life at sea. She nodded sleepily.

"Good morning," she whispered, a small smile playing upon her lips. "I take it that the ale is making a second appearance this morning." He found he was irritated that she seemed to suffer no ill effects of their over-indulgence. In fact, she rather seemed to be glowing, the soft light around her catching the room in streaks of gold and pale blue.

"I suppose I'll have to take back what I said last night," Armand said. She raised an eyebrow, accepting the mug of coffee he offered. "You can most certainly drink *all* the men in London under the table." At that, Catalina took a long drink from her mug.

"It's all about practice," she said. She was just sitting there, the sheet around her waist exposing those two perfect breasts to the room, and Armand was torn between wanting to appease his guilty conscience, and his powerful desire to walk across the room and push her back against the bed, giving him full opportunity to kiss, lick, and bite those delicious pink nipples. He cleared his throat, unsure of what to say next. And then, merely because he could think of no suitable preamble, what with the pounding of rocks against his brain, he came right out and said it.

"I think we should marry."

If she hadn't been bred a noblewoman, he had no doubt that she would have spewed her coffee all over him. As it was, Catalina merely choked on the coffee in her mouth, and then placed the mug down on the bedside table. The calmness with which she moved was far more disorienting than Armand would have cared for.

"I beg your pardon." It had all the ring of a young debutante upon a ballroom floor, but Armand knew better than to believe her. He could feel the stare of a woman who was very accustomed to having her way, and that tone of voice harkened back to their days of youth, when they scampered and scurried their way through the countryside. If Catalina, or Charlotte, did not like something, the casual observer would not have known it from her tone, but anyone the wiser would make haste to hide. As a young girl, Charlotte had a pretty little habit of throwing crockery. Armand was beginning to suspect it was one she hadn't forsaken.

Still, he'd encountered sights far more dangerous than she, even if none were immediately coming to mind. But he set his chin straight and raised one eyebrow in her direction. He longed to close his eyes and wake from this dream, to realize that all of it had been in his mind and that none of it was real. He wasn't supposed to sleep with her. Right now, he only wished he could turn back the clock. He wanted that more than anything.

But it wasn't the truth. He had spent so much time running from his responsibilities, pretending to be someone he was not. This was one matter for which he would need to make amends, to make things right.

"I said—"

But she cut him off. "I know what you said."

By the tone of her voice, he would have assumed all was well, perhaps even expected an acceptance of his proposal. By God, she'd be a fool not to accept it, and Catalina was clearly no one's fool. But there was something akin to steel in her gaze, and Armand felt the rush of last night's alcoholic indulgence all over again, as it tumbled through his stomach. So he offered her a smile, suddenly feeling as though he needed to ward off a coming explosion. He was beginning to get the queer suspicion she was going to say no.

But she didn't say no. In fact, she didn't say anything at all. Instead, Catalina Sol tilted her head back and laughed. She laughed until he could see tears gathering at the corners of her eyes, until her belly rocked and she gripped the sheets. She laughed and she laughed, until Armand could take no more.

"What the hell, Charlotte?"

That stopped her in her tracks. She looked at him. "You're not joking."

It was not a question. Oh, for all that he wanted it to be a question, it was not, and that was most dangerous thing of all.

Still, he answered it regardless, hating the look he now saw in her eyes, hating the fact that she seemed unaware of just how much trouble they had made in giving in to their desires the night before.

He stepped forward, his jaw squared.

"I am most certainly not joking," he said, glad to hear that his voice sounded even and almost calm. For all outward appearances, it might seem that Armand was actually in some sort of control, except a thread of pure rage was climbing up his spine, and he twisted his fingers, his nails cutting into the flesh of his palm. "Charlotte, I don't see what could possibly be funny about this—" Before he could manage his rational argument, as a man should hardly have to give to the woman he had deflowered the evening prior, on exactly why they should wed, she cut him off with a tone so fierce, it stopped his heart for a beat.

"Don't call me that," she said, and it was as though her very voice had turned to ice. "Don't you ever call me that."

Was that it then? Was Lady Charlotte Talbot, daughter of the Earl of Derby, his oldest friend in the world, truly dead?

Before he could ask, however, she continued in her same, steely tone. "I am Catalina Sol, captain of the *Liberté*, and I behave as I please."

He felt a twang of pure fury burning behind his eyes. How it all gone so wrong?

"I eat and drink where I please. I rescue the people I wish to rescue, and I take the lovers I wish to take." Knowing that she had only had the one true lover— himself—the statement should not have made Armand so terrifically angry that she referred to them in plurals, but it did.

"You are ruined." He nearly spat the words, aware that she had gotten under his skin in a way he hadn't allowed anyone to do since youth. Since her. "You are ruined in the eyes of all that matter, and if you do not marry me now, then you will likely never marry anyone."

The expression upon her face almost resembled that of a mother speaking to an insubordinate child, as if the child simply could not comprehend what they were discussing.

"No. I'm not." She was standing now, hurriedly dressing in those tailored britches of hers that had been enticing him for the last few days and pulling her shirt over her head in a rush. He ground his teeth to keep from raising his voice. "I am not ruined from last night because I was ruined far earlier in my life. I will never"—the pause was almost violent—"ever return to society in London. I am Catalina, not Charlotte. Your friend is gone, Armand, and the sooner you understand that, the better we are surely all to be."

"What if you are with child?" he asked her, feeling as though the room were tilting out from below his feet, a sensation which had nothing to do with alcoholic indulgence. "Then what will you do?"

She nearly gaped at him. "Have you not seen the women and children I take in as my own?" she asked. "If I am with child, he or she will have a home as good as any other." Armand's fury was beginning to reach a boiling point, and he was sure his ears were turning red.

"Not the life of an earl's child. Not the life that your child deserves."

She snapped her head around to face him so quickly, he was surprised to see it was still attached. "You do not tell me what sort of life my child does or does not deserve." She was moving and speaking so quickly that Armand was having difficulty keeping her limbs in his line of sight. "If I am with child, I will raise it the way I see fit. And if I am not, then I will return your brother to you and put you on the next passing ship. Or perhaps I'll throw you overboard myself."

They were growing heated regarding their hypothetical offspring, and yet, the idea of a child of Catalina's running roughshod through the Spanish Main, potentially hurting itself, never learning how to be a lord or lady, made Armand's heart ache in a way that angered him all over again.

"You should still marry." He tried to school his voice, but control seemed further out of reach than imaginable. His anger was burning a course through the whole of his body.

"And why on earth should I do that?" She nearly bit him, so quickly did the words spill from her mouth. "If you recall, *my lord*, marriage is the fundamental cause for my running away from London in the first."

That she had him there was not reason enough for Armand to release the topic from his tightly clenched fists. "There are other men," he said. "There are men who will treat you properly, care for you." He was getting dangerously close to a duel, Armand was beginning to think, but still, he could not seem to back down.

"Like you, Armand?" she asked him. Her voice had reached an even tone, with no emotion evident, and that was far more terrifying than her angered yelling. *Like him.* He could have been her husband these years now, had he ever written back, had he not turned himself away from everything London and Paris were to him. He had been a coward and fool.

And yet, the knowledge did not serve to calm his temper in the slightest. Instead, he nearly ground his teeth to dust, as she continued her even speech.

"I have never needed a man to care for me," she said, her gaze so full of disdain, Armand felt himself growing smaller in the wake of it. "I have never needed anyone to care for me." This time, when she spoke, there was no denying the sadness that filtered through her words, or the expression in her eyes, and Armand felt his own grief in it, felt his own sadness as it mirrored hers.

"Why are you trying to change me?" she asked him. He knew he needed to back down, knew that if he spoke right at this moment, as this woman stood before him in her britches, then he would regret it forever. He knew all these things, and yet the anger seemed to consume him, anger, fear, sadness.

"It's about time someone tried."

He watched her finish dressing and leave without another word, but there was no denying the pain he saw in those beautiful eyes, and he felt all the hurt he had caused her as acutely as if someone had dug a knife into his very own body. Of course he didn't want to change her, not the glorious laughter that exposed her long stretch of beautiful neck, not the way she treated the world's misfits, offering them love and joy, so much more than just clothing and food. There was not a single thing in the world he would change about Catalina Sol.

He stopped short, eyes still wide upon the doorway through which she had only just left. If he didn't want to change her, then why had he said so? Why had he said the one thing he knew would hurt her more than all the rest?

Because she had done the same.

She hadn't even said no, hadn't even rejected him in a way that stood to break him, but as Armand stood in Catalina's chamber all alone, he realized he hadn't proposed out of honor. He hadn't suddenly developed the sense of responsibility that had forsaken him all those years ago.

He had proposed because he wanted to marry her. The thought was like a knife turning in his belly, and it sent a shard of new pain through his temple.

He had wanted to marry her.

As she had lain in the morning sunshine, her hair spread around her, that delicious glow upon her skin, Armand had believed it his duty to marry Catalina, but it hadn't been his duty. It hadn't been his responsibility. It had been his desire.

And then she had laughed, had laughed and thrown his betrayal of their once future in his face, and Armand hadn't understood why he had been so angry. But he understood now, he knew exactly what had driven him to say the words he knew would bring her to her knees. Because she had brought him to his knees and Armand Rajaram de Bourbon, earl, *comte*, somewhere in line for an Indian princehood, didn't like the sensation one bit.

Chapter Fifteen

Catalina could count on a single hand the number of times she had cried since leaving London all those years ago. Of the four, in her memory, three had occurred within her first year away, as she longed for her family, for her home, as she had come to understand she could never return. The most recent had been a few years back, when her beloved friend and confidante, a girl by the name of Maggie Hunt, had been lost in a particularly difficult childbirth. That memory still pained her through the night.

She had not cried when she learned she had been officially denounced from society. She had not cried when she had heard of her absentee father's death. But now, as she sat in her chamber, staring out of the large window at the far-off island, the gentle sway of the ship making her stomach churn, Catalina felt the rise of painful, hot tears press against her lids. She had cried for Eliza, to marry a man twice her age. She had cried for Maggie. She would not cry for herself.

But who was *herself*? Long ago, Catalina had believed she would marry. She had dreamed of it, of the little girls and boys who would run between her legs, who she might teach to use a rapier, to a climb a mast. But then she had grown wise to the notion that women who were captains of known almost-pirate ships did not marry, and they certainly didn't bring children into their world. She had learned that, and then set her chin, tied her britches, and never looked back. It hadn't bothered her overmuch, and truth be told, she hadn't thought over the topic in years.

Catalina interrupted her own musings to look out the window once more. Her first mate, Delilah, was perfectly capable of steering the ship toward the far island cove, where their supposed turncoats had told them Henri was being held. She felt a clog in her throat and swallowed a generous sip of brandy straight from the bottle.

She had been happy, until Armand had pointed out the largest flaw in setting off for a life at sea. Who the hell was he, to go about telling her what she ought to be doing or not doing? Who the hell was this man, who had once been a friend so many years ago, storming into her life and demanding that she find some sense of propriety? Catalina let out a very unladylike snort. She'd be damned if she married because someone else wanted her to. The last time that had been asked of her, she had fled the damned country.

But it wasn't so much the marriage proposal that had been haunting her since the ship had set sail that morning. It was his parting words, words, she knew, that were intended to sting with as much power and potency as a scorpion's tail.

Well, it's about time someone tried.

She had thought Armand might be different from the rest. She had thought so at her own peril, allowed him to become a little too close for safety, and now she was paying the price. Another swallow of brandy from the bottle and Catalina bit her lip. Why would he be any different?

Because she had loved him. Once upon a time, as a young green girl of fifteen, she had loved him, and that hadn't been a flight of fancy or some lighthearted lust for her friend, born from convenience and safety. No, she had truly loved him, loved the way his unruly hair had fallen before his eyes, loved the way that he made her laugh, even as he had tried to scold her. She had loved him the way adults love.

Being by his side again, all these years later, after she had fled, after her father died, had dulled the ache in her chest that his absence had brought on, just a little. But then their friendship had begun anew, and the rest of that sadness had melted, the rest of that anger had ebbed, and she had *seen* him again, he and she both so different now, and yet, he had taken her breath away.

Well, not anymore. If she had felt the start of any mad emotion before the night previous, it was surely gone with the morning sun. She could damn well forget about anything that might have to do with Armand being in her future. That wasn't what she wanted, not anymore. And yet, the pain of the realization stung her a thousand times over. She had thought she might have found someone who would accept her for who she was *now*, not who she had been, not who she could be if she put her mind to it. No, Armand was supposed to be different. At least, that was what her heart had been telling her. But he was just like the all the rest. Catalina hated how much that thought burned her through.

****

She told Delilah that she was going alone. The ship had found purchase within a small cove of islands and grottos, and there would be little use in attempting to stage an attack before morning, not with the moon's light hidden behind the clouds, and the ocean so murky and dark. No, it was best she go alone, learn the area, find out what she needed to know. They could return when she had a clear understanding of the pirate location and numbers.

Catalina told her first mate, and only her first mate. Her name was Delilah—at least that's what she had told Catalina—and if her stories of why she had run from home were anything to go by, then she had well enough earned the name. But Catalina loved her frightfully. Tall, buxom, strong as the rum they drank from big, wooden barrels to keep themselves warm on stormy nights, Delilah had a no-nonsense way about her that Catalina could put her full faith into, without pause. They had known each other an age, and Delilah hadn't hesitated a moment when Catalina told her where she was going.

"You'll take a man with ye," Delilah said, her voice reaching with Irish brogue that had taken Catalina months to fully understand. "You're not to go alone onto the island, Captain. I'll be damned if I'll let you do that."

But Catalina was the captain, even if she felt as though she had lost all her control in the world, and ultimately, she convinced her friend that going alone onto the island was exactly what they needed.

"Why can't ye send one of the lads, Captain?"

But she had shaken her head and told Delilah to take care. "If I'm not back by the stroke of midnight, you'll search for me," she said, aware that she was taking a terrible risk entirely for the sake of being off the damned boat where *he* was. She couldn't face him. Not right now.

Well, it's about time someone tried.

"I'll send the hounds," Delilah promised gleefully. Then she had made a distraction large enough for Catalina to shin down one of the thick ropes hanging from the bow and land herself up to the neck in warm salt water, climbing into one of the rowboats Delilah lowered after her. The scabbard Catalina had secured around her shoulder was a comforting weight, the sword across her back and the dagger in her boot reminders that she would always be able to fend for herself, no matter the circumstances.

It felt good to row, to stretch her body to its capacity as she pumped against the current. A physical challenge would always be preferable to an emotional one. Their two turncoat pirates had told them the cave where their crew kept the ransom hostages was in the southernmost point of the second cove of islands and she pushed hard against the murky depths of the ocean. A series of miniscule landings, some no larger than boulders, made for an open ring of islands that narrowed the closer one got to the largest of the chain. The ins and outs of those small islands were riddled with low-tide dwelling carnivores, sharp reefs, and dangerous rocks, but they provided cover and gave the owner of that innermost island a great advantage when it came to greeting unwelcome guests. None of that scared Catalina. She rowed until her cheeks flushed red, rowed until she felt her hair come undone from its braid, pulled apart by the wind swells catching between the coves. She rowed until she saw the telltale light of lanterns filling a cave, their glow bouncing off the stone walls, and what was likely a pile of coins and goblets and jewels.

Catalina hauled her body onto a small rock, secured the rowboat, and took a few deep breaths. She hadn't been lying to Delilah when she said she wasn't going searching for Henri, not necessarily. If she saw him, she would act in accordance with their set of rules, but only if she might also make it out of the pirate's hive alive.

Slowly, she stood, slipping silently from her rock to the next, until she could properly view the scene within the cave. Surely, the cave positively glittered with stolen goods, but it was more the enormous wooden crates that caught her eye, crates that held the seal of the de Bourbon Trade Company stamped upon them, crates that belonged to the man currently tied up beside them, an enormous bull of a pirate standing guard near his feet. Armand had been right. They were holding Henri captive for ransom, but they'd been stealing and diverting his goods as well. For being outlaws, it appeared these pirates were also quite savvy with business.

Henri was so close. She could all but reach her hand out and grab him. She needed to get his attention, to tell him that he wasn't alone. He didn't look as though he'd been treated terribly, but a dark swelling shadowed his eye and his head lolled to the side. Catalina swallowed, her heart pumping with a mixture of potent fear and powerful adrenaline. This was where she belonged. This was the life she wanted to live, saving people who needed saving, taking mad, wild risks. Anyone who couldn't see that didn't know her at all.

Chapter Sixteen

Armand stared at the ceiling above his hammock for three hours before he finally put his feet to the ground. It was useless. He hadn't been able to sleep properly through the night for weeks. What had given him the impression he would pick up the skill now?

Of course, it wasn't the sway of the waves beneath his feet, or even the fear for his brother's safety, that was keeping him from dozing off into the sweet bliss of sleep. No. This was guilt. Pure, raw, gnawing at him like some vicious beast. He had hurt her in a way he hadn't even realized he was capable of, and all because, against his better judgment, he'd begun to care for her.

Damn it all. He didn't want to want her, didn't want to crave the swell of her breast, as it had fit so perfectly in his hand, didn't want his body aching to touch her, to caress each sweet curve of her hip, the delicious weight of her behind, as it had pressed against him. His cock twitched behind his britches, and Armand sighed again. Wanting her was an inconvenience, but it wasn't a disaster.

Caring for her was another matter entirely.

Caring for Catalina Sol could only get him into trouble. It could only mean a lifetime of chasing sails and worrying for her safety. He pursed his lips. Regardless of his own feelings, the guilt wasn't going to disappear until he apologized for being an ass. He *had* been an ass, and she hadn't deserved it. Still, if she didn't marry him, then what the hell was she planning to do if she ever thought to return to London? She was a ruined woman, and he refused to leave her to the wolves. Perhaps out of the small confines of her chamber, she would be more understanding of the situation. Perhaps she would be more inclined to accept his offer. The thought that he felt stung by her rejection was one he pushed soundly out of his mind, as he made his way down the familiar path to her chamber.

Without knowing what he was going to say to the woman who seemed to be haunting his past, present, and future, he knocked soundly upon the door.

There was no response. He knocked again, the guilt in his stomach turning to something altogether more intense, more raw. Still, no response. Without a care to her fury at the destruction of her door, he slammed the wood in with his shoulder until the lock gave.

The room was empty. The sitting desk where he had seen her poring over ledgers by candlelight held no captain. The table was not set. Only a single candle glowed in the room, as if a beacon to return home to.

She could be somewhere else upon the ship, Armand reasoned with himself. She could be anywhere on the grand *Liberté*. But somehow, in the deepest pit of his stomach, he knew the truth.

That was Catalina. She went first. She didn't risk her men or women to scope out an area of danger until she had done so herself. She was no coward, not like him.

Armand took off through the winding hallways of the ship like a man possessed. It wasn't that he didn't trust her. For the first time since their reunion in the vast ocean of the world, Armand realized he trusted her implicitly, trusted her more than he could trust himself, it seemed. No, this feeling had nothing at all to do with trusting her, but rather the roiling, uncomfortable sensation in his gut that *something was wrong*. They had been docked within the island cove for more than three hours, and Catalina had likely been gone the entire time. If she were only on a scouting mission, then it didn't make sense to be gone so very long.

He found the first mate, a large woman named Delilah, asleep in a hammock below stairs, and he shook her, all his fear and concern going into the hands that now trembled before him.

"Apologies for the rude awakening," he told her, in a tone that was equally requiring of an apology. "I was hoping you might be able to discern the location of your captain." For a moment, she looked confused, and the question seemed to register.

"What time is it?" Delilah asked. She was not a woman who panicked easily. No one aboard the *Liberté* panicked easily, except, it appeared, Armand. Still, Delilah had an expression upon her face that only served to fuel the fire of his fears.

"Half past twelve," he told her, after a quick glance at his pocket watch. She jumped from the hammock with a skill only obtained from months of living in one.

"It's been too long," Delilah said, her voice rising slightly in alarm. "Captain told me to come after her if she weren't back by midnight." Armand resisted the urge to yell at the first mate. Catalina running off to do exactly what she wanted to do was not something anyone was able to stop.

"Well, it's past that time, certainly," he said, but

already he was climbing the stairs to the deck and calling over his shoulder. "Collect your best fighters. We'll split into a team and take half of them to find the captain. The other half will remain here to guard the ship." Delilah was nothing if not a capable first mate, and within moments, half a dozen crewmembers stood before Armand.

He looked them over, his mind only half able to concentrate, as he considered all the ways Catalina might have gotten herself into danger. He tried to reassure himself. She was perfectly capable of taking care of herself. The last weeks in her company had surely proven that. But now he felt as though he had been dropped off at sea with a rock tied around his ankle. Something about this woman grated on him. She made him crazy, made him want to tear his hair from his head, made him want to shove her against the nearest wall and kiss her senseless. There was no denying, despite his feelings, that she was a powerful, capable woman.

Catalina would be fine. Armand would make damned sure of it.

After a moment's choice, he took Delilah, a thin woman named Molly who was apparently famed for her swordsmanship, and two of the larger male members of the crew, Richard and George. The remaining crewmembers were to stay behind and guard the ship. If Catalina returned, they would sound the special wooden whistle with the bird song, intended to attract only the right attention, and the rescue team would return without another thought.

Thus, not ten minutes after rounding up his crew of misfit mercenaries, Armand found himself rowing through the shallow waters of a godforsaken island cove in the middle of the ocean, wet with the spray of sea brine and brimming over with anger. How dare she run off without giving anyone but her first mate notice? And how dare she go without any auxiliary support? If she thought she was being brave, then she was a fool. There was nothing brave in sacrificing yourself without need.

Still, the sensation he had felt only a few hours earlier, as she had laughed at his marriage proposal, returned in full force. Armand tried to reason with himself. He was worrying because she was an old friend. He was worrying because they had a history. He was worrying because they had slept together.

The wooden oar pressed hard into his palm, as Armand and Delilah set the small rowboat full of their rescue team around to the other end of the island chain. But the bite of pain didn't distract Armand from the lie he was trying to tell himself. All those facts remained true, of course. They were old friends with a history who had, in fact, slept together only one night previous. But that wasn't the cause of the intense ache he felt deep in his stomach. No. Armand couldn't shake the feeling that, if anything happened to Catalina, the world would be a much dimmer place.

He hadn't wanted to marry her out of some sense of duty or their shared childhood. He had wanted to marry her because he had wanted to marry her. He wanted to be with her, to see her raise young, dark-haired children that raced around her ankles on the deck of the ship. Armand had long believed that marriage was not the life for him, but seeing Catalina in her full force, taking her all night long, had been enough to convince him that marrying her was something he needed to do.

His thoughts, traitorous as they were, were cut short by the sight of candlelight pouring from an opening in the rock. A metal stake had been forced between two boulders, and they tied the rowboat's rope around it, before climbing up onto a series of rocks that sat just near the cave's opening.

It was a strange space to pick, or the pirates had chosen in a hurried fashion, for instead of just a single opening, as most caves were wont to have, this one had two, as if the back wall had been blown out by an explosion.

Taking a glance at the crew of pirates, Armand considered the idea that it was more than likely these men *had* accidentally blown a hole in their own hideout. The four others followed him, and they were soon all sitting upon the rock, with a good view of the whole cave at large, of the overflowing piles of gold and jewels, the laughing pirates, the movement in the far corner where the cave let out again, and—

He'd be damned. He'd be damned again to hell for murdering her, also. A flash of dark gold hair caught the glimmer of candlelight, and Armand nearly cursed aloud. It would serve her right, getting captured, he thought, with not a small measure of visceral rage. But the sensation of pure panic that filled his chest at the thought was enough to dilute his anger. It didn't matter. He'd give her a stern talking to later. For right now, the focus of their mission was to get to the other side of the pirate hideout and steal back their captain without a single brutal, bloodthirsty pirate noticing. Well, that seemed easy enough.

****

Catalina glanced at Henri, taking stock of his pallor and closed eyes, then darted her attention back to the raucous crowd of pirates laughing around piles of treasures and jugs of ale. She could only just make out a long table, constructed of a board over several barrels. Huge chests, overflowing with ladies' gowns, parasols, and wide-brimmed hats were stacked against one of the walls of the cave. Beside them was a pile of desks and chairs, in beautiful, dark wood—expensive pieces, stacked like lumber for the fire. These men had gone into houses and estates and taken whatever treasures or valuables their grubby hands could carry out.

There would be no stealth here. Between the chests of drawers, piles of coins, and immovable stack of chairs and dresses, and the guards stationed, she had no hope of sneaking about. Too many of them guarded the cave walls and openings. Henri, from his appearance, would not likely be able to move fast enough for a rushed escape. He obviously needed a solid meal, and Catalina was certain she couldn't carry them both off without help. She was strong, but slight and the de Bourbon brothers were a large species of man.

No, she couldn't sneak her way in and out of this hole. Whatever she did was going to have to be dramatic and wild and utterly out of her mind. For a moment, Catalina considered retreating. What the hell did she think to do by walking into a den of pirates, armed with nothing but a sword, a dagger, and her wits? Fair point to her, she could best them to a man with her wits, but that wasn't a fight she'd be having this evening. Damn it all to hell, she should have brought help.

For a moment, her heart thumping so loudly in her chest she was sure they would discover her, Catalina wondered what time it was. She had told Delilah to search for her after the stroke of twelve, but it was a decent distance from the ship, and what if the search party had gone in the wrong direction? She couldn't even be certain it *was* after twelve, and Catalina felt her stomach lurch a little. Henri was so damnably close. Were the gods playing some foul trick upon her?

Henri's mouth seemed to quirk up a little at the corner, though his eyes remained shut, and the action reminded Catalina of just how similar he had always looked to Armand. *Armand.* Her heart seized a little, and she tried to push the distracting thought away. Still, he had always been the clever one, when it came to their tricks in childhood. She'd storm in, wild and excitable, and he would lower his head and widen his eyes and give off every air of an innocent child. Armand was a terrible liar, so Catalina would weave stories of their afternoons, innocent, well-behaved stories, before whatever governess or maid was responsible for them and Armand would bat those long, dark lashes and very nearly always get them out of trouble. If only she had him with her right now. He would be the help she needed to get everyone she had sworn to protect out of this cave alive, including herself.

But there was no more time for delay. It was time to do something—something outrageous, something worthy of the old pirate tales and shanties. At that moment, it occurred to her. The idea was as foolish as the day was long and would almost certainly result in her somehow getting injured or, at the very least, shot at, but she had to do *something* or she would be wasting her very precious chance.

She glanced around and spied a rock coated in seaweed and moss. Draping the plant generously in her hair and across her arms, Catalina stood and walked toward the closest lantern. It was located just below a large rock, and when she stood before it, the light cast her silhouette in an enormous shadow upon the wall.

"Who dares to wake the goddess Calypso?" she roared from atop her perch upon the rock. The room echoed her voice with a powerful ring, and the cave went silent. Mugs stopped in midair, bawdy songs left with the final note unsung, as three-dozen pirates suddenly all turned in her direction. Catalina grimaced. She was in too deep now not to immediately begin swimming.

"I repeat my question." Her voice was positively booming now, for she had found that it was particularly acoustic in her small corner of the cove. "Who dares to wake the sea goddess Calypso?" With all eyes trained upon her, Catalina lifted her arms high, and the shadows danced upon the wall. "You have stolen my lover." The final word rang in the silent, charged air. "And for that, you will all suffer." Where the hell was she going with this? She was aware there was a general sense of restlessness at the table just a few meager feet from where she stood, putting on the world's maddest masquerade.

"Return him to me and cease your ways, or I shall cast you all to the sea with great joy."

She heard a murmur, as one pirate whispered loudly to another, "What do we do? Where's the boy? We've angered the sea goddess!" General flummery of

141

the same sort followed.

"Do as I say, and no harm shall come to thee," she bellowed. "If you disobey me, hell will rain down upon thee." Her heart was pounding with all the force of a military drum in full thunder, and still, the image of Henri lying against the rock, the thought of Armand declaring it was time someone *tried*, was enough to fuel her madness. For certainly, this was madness. She was completely mad.

Well, whatever method was most effective.

"Should we bring him to her?" said a nervous-sounding pirate, whose voice cracked on the high end.

Perhaps she had underestimated their adherence to folklore. Well, that could only work in her favor.

"The captain's keeping him for ransom," another replied, though his words held a note of doubt.

"We'll find another ransom," a third voice put in.

Really, it was a matter of miracles that they had even managed to capture Henri in the first place.

"Bring me the man," she said, fluttering the seaweed before the lantern to spectacular effect, "or I shall cast a spell that marks you all as the next souls to perish at sea."

The first pirate who had spoken made no effort to hide his voice now. "She's talking about the Sea Devil, she is," he said in a squeak. "I don't care 'bout no captain. She can have the man." And he stood from the table so quickly, he knocked over a pile of jeweled serving platters. They hit the ground with a resounding *crash*, and Catalina knew she was beginning to lose her audience.

"My patience is thinning," she said. "If I do not receive the man in a minute's time, I shall damn you all to a watery hell." There was a flurry of activity.

"He's right there," the first pirate squawked. "Over by the chest, do you see?" She turned with a great flourish, as though she hadn't been scoping out Henri's location for the better part of an hour.

"Bring him to me." The room quieted again. "Now." This was beginning to grow rather enjoyable.

Two enormous men untied Henri's bonds and brought him to the base of the rock. Henri blinked his eyes open, looking up at her with marked confusion, as if he were witnessing a play and had just been asked to join the actors upon the stage. She gave him a friendly smile, and he blinked as if he had seen a ghost pass before his very wide eyes. Well, now was no time to explain how the de Bourbon brothers' past had resurfaced.

"Recall your promise to the sea queen, and I shall keep you from harm," Catalina continued, now stepping down from her position atop the high rock. The trick here was going to be getting Henri, who was, thankfully, somewhat more conscious in all the confusion, into the rowboat and back to the ship. It wouldn't do to rescue him from pirates just to let him drown. Still, he was in her care, and that had been the fundamental step.

In fact, she was almost beginning to feel a sense of relief cross over her, as she walked down the steps, her moss- and seaweed-covered form enough to pass before the idiot pirates. She focused on handling Henri's weight, supported upon her shoulder but with great difficulty. In a second, Catalina realized her mistake in believing them out of danger, and all it took was the piercing and all-too-familiar sound of a bullet whistling through still air.

"What in the name of hell and the devil is going on?" came a previously unheard voice, and Catalina turned to the far entrance of the cave, an opening at the other end that she had not before seen. Her heart stopped beating for a full breath, frozen behind her chest in fear. From one captain to another, there was no denying this man was in full custody of his pirate crew and far less credulous of shadow puppets and folktales.

"It's Calypso, it is, Captain," came a voice from the long table, and Catalina was torn between trying to make her escape, far slower for the full-grown male perched upon her shoulder, or keeping her focus squared firmly upon the increasingly irate pirate captain.

"Did you just say *Calypso*?" the captain asked in a voice that would have been considered kind to anyone with the average intelligence of a sea urchin, which was, apparently, the majority of his crew.

"Aye, it was she," another voice put in, "said we stole her lover, she did. Promised to curse us for all time if we didn't return him. She said she'd send us straight to the ocean's bottom, she did."

Catalina was of the firm belief that if men could spit fire, this pirate captain would be a prime candidate for the position. She began to inch toward the opening of the cave, but without much recourse. After all, what would she do upon reaching the water? No doubt they could row their own boats with several men each much faster than she could do all on her own, especially with the added weight of a near unconscious man.

"Well then, *Calypso*…" The captain's focus was now entirely upon her. "Shall we have a little chat regards rules of ownership then?" When she didn't reply, he continued. "As I see it, you've taken something of mine, and I would like it back."

Catalina squared her shoulders, grateful for the shadows of the cove, which helped to hide her from his voice.

"And as I see it, you took something of mine first," she replied. She was both pleased and surprised to hear how steady her own voice was. It wouldn't do much good for the sea goddess to get cold feet.

"Possession is nine tenths of the law," the captain said. Catalina laughed, forcing a bellowing, echoing sound around the cave, while she repositioned Henri upon her shoulder.

"And I possess," she replied. "But, please, challenge my strength—at your own risk, naturally." That was a dangerous move, but it would give her the advantage, if he decided to show his hand to fearing her.

"Do you know who your lover is?" the captain asked, trying a new tack. "He's the younger owner of the de Bourbon Trade Company. I intend to hold him until the elder brother hands the company over to me. I will not allow you take my hostage from me." At this, he lunged forward, and Catalina had only enough time to lower Henri to the ground, and none too gently, before she unsheathed her sword and caught the pirate captain's attack in a fierce parry.

"Do not test your luck with me," she snarled, now able to see his face in the lantern light, one long scar dragging his skin from corner to corner.

"I need no luck," he said with another parry. "I shall wager upon my skill alone."

At that, Catalina brought forward a blow that dazed him for a breath, and she withdrew her sword enough to gain the upper ground.

"You know who he is," she said through clenched teeth. "But do you know who I am?" She pushed off another attack with ease, and the captain finally looked up at her, catching the sight of the woman who had become notorious across the Caribbean. He fell back a step, and she cocked her head to one side.

"I find myself pleased to learn you fear me and my crew more than the sea nymph, herself," she said. "I shall be going now." At that, she turned to lift Henri, turned her back for the single second that made all the difference, and all hell broke loose.

There was an incredible shout, and Armand, Delilah, and a few other members of her crew jumped from the shadows and rushed toward her with a battle cry. Armand caught the captain's sword with his own, and Catalina realized she had just given a pirate the perfect target, her exposed back. With Armand keeping the man busy in a dalliance of swords, she carefully supported Henri down the rocky steps. To her immense relief, the entrance to the cave where her crewmembers had been hiding held several rowboats, two of which belonging to her ship, the other likely to the captain.

With a few swift movements, she managed to get Henri into the water long enough to reach the boat. She deposited him with little fanfare, accepted his grateful smile, and turned back toward the fray.

Armand struggled fiercely against the captain, pushing back the pirate's sword with the blunt angle of his own, before the sharp side sliced his jaw. As Catalina's gaze darted around, taking in the scrimmages and shouts of pain and anger, it become all too clear they were outnumbered. Her crew had come on a search party, not a rescue mission.

Well, it was too late to think much on it. Now, she simply needed to ensure their safe return to the ship. She slashed, sliced, kicked, and yelled, and a few minutes later, she had managed to collect all her crew, excepting Armand who was still in a fierce lock with the pirate captain. He had one hand around the other man's wrist and was trying to break loose his grip on the sword, but the captain struggled and hissed and did not give an inch. Something flickered in of the corner of her eye, and Catalina chanced a single glance, to find a pile of pistols glinting in the glow of the lamplight. She dove for it, darting behind a chest of clothing and jewels, and took a pistol in both hands. The silver chasing glinted again in her grip, but not the way it had before. This wasn't the glisten of a single lamp against the shine of her gun. Frantic, she turned her head.

She saw it before Armand, but a moment later, realization flickered in his eyes. The last time she had seen that expression on his face, Armand had been recalling the pirate ship burning like the flames of hell, taking his mother down to a watery beyond.

Fire. Fire lapped at the corners of the cave, spilling across the room like a midnight spook from beneath the bed. Fire crept, and it slunk, and it roared into the room, almost as if sound had paused, only to return in a great thundering rage. Fire brought two very real, very immediate problems. One was in the form of a massive stack of wooden barrels pressed against the far end of the cave and undoubtedly filled with gunpowder. The other was in the form of her oldest friend.

147

Armand had never been able to countenance fire. Not since it had stolen his mother from him, not since the day it had torn his family apart. This great hulking, powerful man froze in his place, as though he had stared down the eyes of Medusa herself. Only it wasn't Medusa before him, but an enraged pirate captain with a sword coming down on Armand's throat.

Catalina Sol didn't like to kill. But in some cases, killing might be the only way to save someone from certain death. She gripped the pistol. The captain's hands went up, and he brought the sword up for leverage, ready to slice his opponent. Armand crumpled to the ground before the captain got the chance, felled like a giant tree in the forest, his eyes glazed with the palpable fear she knew to be his very worst. With the captain's hand raised, arm exposed, Catalina took her opportunity where she saw it. She lifted her gun, aimed at his heart, and shot.

Time slowed, as if they were moving through molasses. The bullet struck him straight in the chest, and a bright bloom of red began to unfurl across his dirty white shirt. Catalina couldn't hear. The only sound in the room was the *rat tat tat* of her own heart pounding against her bones. She raced over to where Armand lay upon a rock, his body crumpled from the shock of the fire raging around them. Her heart wrung with the fear he might have hit his head, might have been injured beyond hope. Her fear for his life ran parallel with the need to get them *out* before the growling, hungry flames made it to the back end of the cave and took them all out in the process. Without thought to the dying pirate, she kneeled before Armand, and that was her mistake.

The knife caught her in the side. Likely, the captain had been aiming for her neck, but the sound of him sliding to the cave ground with a tremendous *crash* came only a split second after the roaring pain filled her ears, piercing and overwhelming her senses. Yet all she could think about was Armand. Was he all right? Was he alive? That was all that mattered. And then Armand was smiling, and he picked her up, even as the room seemed to fade and the edges of her view grew misty with shadows spiderwebbing across her vision. She felt the low rocking of water, and then a wild, incredible reverberation rocked the world. But it slowed, and so did Catalina's thoughts. They had Henri, and the pirate captain was dead. All was well.

Chapter Seventeen

Catalina stirred, and Armand jumped from his chair, only to watch her mouth close and her eyes remain shut. Three hours. Three hours since they had pulled the dagger from her side, and she had not woken. The blood loss was overwhelming, and with each moment that passed, Armand's heart sank deeper into his stomach, as if a great anchor were pulling it down. Across the room, Henri lay stretched out upon another cot, but he was sitting up against the wall, eating a bowl of soup, and watching the two of them.

She had saved his brother. She had nearly gotten herself killed. She might *have* gotten herself killed. The thought that they were not yet out of the woods was like a rush of hot fiery fear. She needed to be alive because he had to apologize for saying he wanted to change her. What in hell could he have been thinking, saying a fool thing like that? The woman who lay on the cot before him, bandaged side, seaweed-covered hair and all, had nothing about her that needed changing. She was perfect. She had rushed in, headstrong and utterly cracked, and she had saved his brother, just as she had promised him. She had saved them all.

And now. Well, now she was going to die for it. That simply couldn't be. Armand's mind was aflame with the molten rage of it. He wouldn't let it. He had to apologize. He had to thank her for saving his life, for knowing the one thing about him that he had never told anyone—the deepest fear he had never needed to say aloud for her to know. He had to tell her the truth—she didn't have a damn thing about her that anyone should change. The truth was he didn't want to marry her out of some sense of propriety and righteousness. The truth was he loved her.

It struck him sideways, like a great wave crashing against a hull. He loved her. He loved her with a ferocity that scared him; he loved her in a way that transcended everything else. If she wanted to return to London, he would follow. If she wished to remain a captain for the rest of her days, he would beg the honor of being her first mate. Because Armand had been falling for her, despite his best intentions, since the day she had walked back into his life, since she had shaken his bed by night and his soul by day, since she had saved his brother, since she had saved him. The only trick now was convincing her of the fact and hoping she survived long enough to try.

****

Catalina was on a boat. Was she on a boat? Her head seemed to be shifting up and down, as if riding the waves beneath. It didn't feel like a boat. Inside her own head, her mind was cresting and riding enormous waves, painful, brightly lit waves that hurt to stare at for too long.

She could fall off the boat right now, couldn't she? The water would swallow her whole, and she could slip away into its depths and allow herself to ease the pain. Since leaving home, there had always been a little bit of pain, and though she pushed it far away, it never truly disappeared. Home. Where was home again? She

151

searched for a place in her aching mind, but all she could manage was the image of a man. His dark hair nearly fell to his shoulders, but his face calmed her and lessened the painful thudding of her mind. She knew that man. She knew him from an age ago, knew a man who looked just like him, this one from not so long before she had found herself on a boat off at sea.

And then she heard a voice far off in the distance. Had the man called her? Surely not. He must have heard the call as well, because he turned in her direction, and when she caught his gaze, stark against the white foggy background of the sea outside the ship, Catalina knew exactly who the stranger was. He was the man who had saved her life. Or had she saved his? He was the man she had grown up with when they had been children, the man she had fallen in love with even before she had been old enough to understand what love was. He was speaking now, his voice mouthing words she couldn't quite understand, as if he were whispering below the surface of the water upon which they rode. She called to him, begged him to say his words again.

"Come back, Charlotte," he said.

Charlotte. Who was Charlotte? Yet it seemed to make sense that he would call her Charlotte. More words spilled from his mouth, not quite meeting the rhythm of his lips as they did. Was his hair on fire? He didn't appear fazed by the idea.

"Christ, Charlotte," he was saying now, though his hair was most definitely burning. "I'm the worst sort of fool for what I said to you. You need to come out of this so I can explain." Come out of what? They were standing upon a ship together, and the ocean around them was glowing. Everything was so bright, and the waves appeared to catch the sky and pull it closer. She reached for his hand, and their fingers brushed. Whatever happened, whether she fell to the sea or not, she couldn't be there without him. He would be her lifeline to safety, the closest thing to a rescue mission she had ever known. He would take her home, to the home that was *him*. If he fell from this ship, she would follow without question.

Because she loved him. The thought seemed to imprint itself against the bright white sky. She did love him, didn't she, Catalina thought with a detached sense of understanding. She had always loved him. But this new version of him, this wild man who had carried her from the pirate cave, who had made love to her all night long and then proposed because he believed it to be the right thing to do, the man who had forsaken all responsibilities that had been given to him and taken up the ones he had been forced to earn, this man was truly the one worth loving.

His fingers seemed to be sliding out of her grasp. They were so hot they burned her like boiling water, and Catalina began to panic. He couldn't disappear, not when she was only just beginning to understand what he meant to her. She gripped harder, aware that he was slipping away, right out of the picture, in fact. And so she screamed, screamed his name loud enough for the whole world to hear, because he couldn't leave, because what would she be without him?

****

Catalina woke in a cold sweat. Her body was shaking, and the alarming sound that had woken her had, in fact, come from her very own mouth. With a start, she snapped it shut, an action that sent a pulse of painful irritation right through her sensitive head.

What the devil? Belatedly, she realized a thick blanket lay over her, and she pulled it tight to her body, aware that she felt too cold and too hot all at once, aware that *something was wrong*. Where was she? Where was the man who had been in her dreams?

"Catalina?"

She looked up to a familiar face, which brought such a rush of relief, Catalina nearly wept.

"Antonia," she said, her voice a mixture of confusion and comfort. "What happened? Where am I?"

Concern crossed her friend's face, but then she covered it in an instant. "You're at Dwyer, love," Antonia said sweetly, brushing back a piece of Catalina's hair that had stuck to her cheek. "You gave us all quite a fright." Catalina looked up, feeling like a small child. Had she really wanted to do this alone? Had she really and truly wanted to be so independent as to never ask for help? With the sweet face of her friend looking down upon her, Catalina could see no reason to lie to herself. Before she managed to answer her own musing, however, Antonia continued.

"You've been battling a fever some eight days now, Catalina," she said. She sat beside Catalina's bed and began sponging cold water across her forehead. "We weren't quite certain you would, well…" Antonia looked down at her feet rather than continue. "But it appears you have. You must be starved. I'll fetch some soup and fresh water." She stood up and was halfway toward the door before turning back around.

"There's someone who wishes to see you," she said

with a small smile. Catalina couldn't quite figure out what that smile meant, but she was too tired to dwell and instead settled back into bed. The image of Armand had all but fled her memory, or dream, or whatever it had been, but the fear remained in the pit of her belly. She had lost him. Eight days, and all she could remember was the searing pain of a dagger going through her skin and muscle, and then nothing. Eight days. A man could travel far in eight days.

She had rejected him. Why on earth had she done that? It was difficult to think. The pain in her side and the fuzziness in her head sent her focus just outside of where she could grasp it, and yet, Catalina knew she had made a mistake. It was a matter of determining what that mistake was.

There was a knock on the door, and when Catalina called for entrance, her heart nearly flew from her chest. He hadn't left. He was here, in her home for lost souls, and he stood before her with a smile that made Catalina wonder just how close to death's doorstep she had come.

"You gave me a fright," Armand said. He sat down beside her, and Catalina realized with a start that he had been in her dream because he had been here beside her. His presence in the small chair was right, it was familiar, it had remained by her side for the eight days of her lingering fever. *He* had stayed by her side. That was a terribly important fact, and she pushed it into the forefront of her mind.

"Henri?" she mumbled.

Armand's smile widened. "More than well," he told her. "I believe he's chatting up your Antonia as we speak."

Her heart still hammered. "And the pirates."

Armand nodded. "Blown to bits, from what we saw. The fire must had reached their gunpowder stock, and the whole cave collapsed."

A sense of satisfaction washed over Catalina, and she finally turned to the most important matter of all. Managing a small smile, she said, "You stayed."

He placed his hand upon hers. "I couldn't leave you," he replied.

She recoiled. He felt guilty that she had been injured. It was his damned sense of honor coming through again. But then his fingers were stroking her damp skin, and Catalina felt the cool sense of relief that came with his touch.

"I don't wish to marry you," Armand said.

She blinked. She thought her grasp on the reality increasing, but apparently, a chapter had been skipped in the book.

He grinned at her expression. "I don't wish to marry you because you don't wish to marry me."

This was important. Images of that morning when they had shared her chamber on board the ship, of her realizing he only wanted to marry her because it was the *right thing to do*, flashed before her mind. If only she could tell him she had changed her mind. If only she could explain she had never ever wanted to be someone's burden, someone's responsibility. If only he understood she needed to be the master of her own fate.

"I was a fool, Catalina," Armand said, his hands never leaving hers, their weight a welcome warmth. "I should have known better than to try and change you."

The words were familiar, and she realized he must have said them time and again while she slept through her waxing and waning fever.

He shook his head, presumably at his own stupidity. "It turns out the best parts of you are the ones that drive me the craziest. The madder and more dangerous you are, the more I find myself falling in love with you."

Catalina sat straight up. "You love me," she whispered, her heart beating a mad rhythm.

His grin widened. "It's been a long time coming, has it not?"

Catalina shook her head. "You don't love me," she said, convinced of the truth of it. "You think I'm brash and irresponsible and wild and dangerous."

He nodded. "All of those things and more," he told her. "Mad, insubordinate, and completely unaware of what you do to me."

The honesty in his words made her stomach flip, and this time it came out as a question. "You love me?"

Because she had begun to understand it was all the craziest, most maddening parts of him she couldn't live without. He was temperamental and straight-laced and responsible and damning of his reputation and all sorts of things that had been riding her since the start. But those were all the traits she found she most longed for. Those, and his deep, powerful kisses.

"I love you, Catalina Sol," Armand said, squeezing her hands in his. "And I've been too much of a blind man to admit it. Then we almost lost you, and I knew I couldn't be any sort of man at all, without you. I don't know what I would become if I never got to tell you how I feel."

Catalina's smile was painful, but she barely felt it. "Armand," she whispered in wild excitement.

157

He nodded.

"I think I love you too." She said it again, for the sheer sake of feeling the words upon her tongue. "I do. I most definitely do love you. I didn't want to, but then you followed me and saved my life, and I understood you were the support I was most hoping for. I realized in my dreams that if you disappeared, I'd be disappearing with you."

Armand placed a chaste, sweet kiss up on her lips. "I'm not going to ask you to marry me," he repeated. "Because I know you don't want me to ask." He took a deep breath. "I'm going to ask you to simply be with me." He released a low, pent-up sigh. "Please? I don't think I can live without you."

She shook her head, aware that tears were beginning to pool behind her eyelids.

"Will you marry me?" she blurted out from behind her hands. "Marry me, Armand. Be my magistrate husband and tame my seafaring ways. Marry me, Armand Rajaram de Bourbon."

The sheen in his eyes made the back of her own feel hot and overwhelmed with joy, a sensation echoed deep in her heart.

He nodded, and then he cupped her in his enormous embrace, and the sheer power of his clasp was at once overwhelming and perfect.

"Yes," he whispered in her ear. "Yes, I'll marry you."

****

A few weeks passed before the surgeon declared Catalina fit to return to normal life. The dagger wound in her side no longer threatened her life. Antonia had acted like a bustling mother hen, until Armand had taken over the role, and she was desperate to get a chance to stretch her sore limbs and feel fresh air.

The sun was just rising over the horizon line, when Catalina donned a thin linen shirt and pair of light britches. She left her boots off, preferring the feel of the cool stone floor upon her feet, and then she slipped from the house and into the back garden.

The garden was lovely. Rows and rows of vegetables twinkled with morning dew. Catalina breathed in the fresh sea air, and the whole world came alive around her. How could it not? She loved the man who loved her back. He loved her back. The thought was no less intoxicating for the number of times she repeated it.

In a fit of joy, she planted herself upon a patch of cool grass and looked up to the sky. Light lavender clouds were just beginning to part, in favor of the early morning blue. A small noise sounded nearby, breaking through the calm of the morning. Catalina went to roll up, her instincts kicking in as fast as her panic at recalling that she hadn't brought her weapons outside.

But then all fear faded as she saw her fiancé standing before her, blocking the early sunrise from her eyes.

"Hello, Captain," Armand said. His voice was husky and promising, and Catalina felt herself throb at the hitch in his words. "Reporting for duty."

She grinned, holding out her hand and guiding him to lie next to her in the damp grass. Armand de Bourbon, earl and business owner, lying on the wet ground. It was a funny thing indeed.

"Henri is recovering nicely," he told her, folding his hands behind his head to look up at the sky. Then he turned to face her. "I owe you everything, Catalina." It was the second most powerful thing he had said to her, with the sole exception of *I love you.*

"Antonia enjoys fussing over him," she replied, enjoying the lazy circles he was drawing upon her skin, where her linen shirt had ridden up, or rather, been pulled up. "I'm sure the fact that he's so devilishly handsome could contribute to her pleasure." Teasing Armand was certainly contributing to her own.

"Wench," he growled into her ear, his tongue just ghosting over her skin. She suppressed a shudder of desire. It never did any good for your opponent to know how much control he had over you. But then his mouth was roaming over her chest, kissing the curves of her collarbones and sliding down between the open flap of her shirt.

"Sails are raised?" She said it as a question, but the firm press of his delicious cock against her thigh was answer enough. He bit her for the terrible joke, but then slid his hand over the curve of her bottom, pressing her thighs against his body.

"Permission to come aboard, Captain?" he asked fiercely. She was panting into his mouth now and thoroughly enjoying his hand cupping her breast through the shirt.

"Permission granted," she whispered. And he did just that.

Epilogue

20 May 1806
London

"It's beautiful," Catalina said. "I couldn't be happier." She turned to face her husband and took his hands in her own. "Armand, it's perfect. Thank you." She placed a fierce kiss upon his lips. "May we go inside?"

He nodded, his eyes following the quick-footed two-year-old who had escaped her mother's clutches in her moment of excitement.

And so they entered the London townhouse previously of the Earl of Devon, and now the twice-as-large London townhouse of the earls of Devon and Derby, now known as the Liberté Home. It was enormous, and the workers, whom Armand had handpicked for the job, had done remarkable work of connecting the two homes so they appeared as if it had never been any other way.

"There are four dormitories," he said, as they entered the main foyer of the house. "Split between boys and girls, men and women. I've had the workshops set up across the first floor. Anamitra, don't touch that!" He followed their young daughter, who had already absconded with a long piece of wood she had found left over from the construction.

161

Catalina was walking into one of the workshops now, a room with several enormous weaving looms positioned in long rows. She clapped her hands together again, feeling as though she might burst into tears. She hugged Ana and Armand close to her body.

"Now, Henri and Antonia have promised to keep Dwyer House running in full working order"—he looked at her with a melting grin that didn't promise overmuch for her britches—"and we've our responsibilities upon the *Liberté*, so I took the liberty of finding the proper person to keep charge of the house."

She raised her eyebrow. For so many years she had done it all on her own. She was still not used to Armand putting his hand in. She didn't have long to wait, however, because the front door opened again behind them, and—

"Eliza!" Catalina squealed, and her sister rushed into her embrace with the force of a tidal wave.

"Charlotte..." Eliza held her at arm's length to take her in fully. "Caterina?"

Catalina shook her head, wiping away the tears that had traitorously escaped. "Catalina," she said weepily. "Eliza." She took a step back and looked at her grown sister. Eliza was a woman now, a beautiful, bright, delicious woman. Catalina stepped back and gave Ana a gentle touch. "This is your Aunt Eliza," she said.

Eliza cooed over the young girl, before turning back to Catalina.

"You're to be our house manager, then?" she asked, unable to keep the tears at bay.

Eliza nodded with excitement. "I'm still in my mourning period, and there's very little I'm allowed to do by societal rules." She laughed at Catalina's obvious

162

expression of distaste for society's rules. "But there's plenty I can do to prepare for opening the home." She looked at the three of them, then gathered Catalina's and Armand's hands into her own. "She always said she would marry you," Eliza told her brother-in-law with pure joy in her voice.

Armand smiled, a warm, melting smile to Catalina's mind, and then turned to face her. "Then I am all the more foolish for having waited so long to return her affections," he said, in that deep tone of his. "But we have no worry of that anymore, have we, Captain?"

She shook her head, the sensation of a warm glow deep in her belly all too impossible to ignore. Their affections for each other had only grown and strengthened these last years, proof of which was swimming around in her belly and most certainly the cause for her teariness. But she would tell him later.

For now, Catalina was simply happy to stand in their new home for wayward souls, her dearest sister, her loving husband, and her darling daughter, together—a true family again at last.

A word about the author…

Holland Rae is the author of several works of erotic and romantic fiction in both the contemporary and historical genres and enjoys pushing the limits of freedom, feminism, and fun in her stories. She has been an avid writer for many years and recently moved back to her home state of New Jersey from Boston, after completing her education in journalism and creative writing.

In her free time, she loves to travel and spent several months living in a 14th-century castle in the Netherlands. When not exploring the world, she likes dreaming up stories, eating spicy food, driving fast cars, and talking to strangers.

Find Holland on
Facebook: https://www.facebook.com/HollandRae/
Twitter: https://twitter.com/@RaeRomance/
Pinterest: https://www.pinterest.com/hollandraeroman/
Instagram: https://www.instagram.com/hollandraeromance/
Or at https://HollandRae.com